The Street

The Street

A NOVEL BY
Israel Rabon

TRANSLATED FROM THE YIDDISH AND
WITH AN AFTERWORD BY
LEONARD WOLF

FOUR WALLS EIGHT WINDOWS
NEW YORK

First paperback printing, November 1990
Originally published by Schocken Books, 1985
English translation © 1985 by Leonard Wolf.
All Rights Reserved.

Library of Congress Cataloging-in-Publication Data:

Rabon, Israel, b. 1900.
    [Gas. English]
    The street : a novel / by Israel Rabon ; translated from the
Yiddish and with an afterword by Leonard Wolf.
      p. cm.
    Translation of: Di gas.
    ISBN 0-941423-45-X : $9.95
    I. Title.
[PJ5129.R217G313   1990]
839'.0933—dc20   90-14113
                                                      CIP

Four Walls Eight Windows
P.O. Box 548
Village Station
New York, New York 10014

Printed in the U.S.A.

The Street

Prologue

Eight weeks ago I was released from my army service. It was a rainy summer day at the end of July when I ate my last meal as a soldier in the 27th Infantry Regiment in Tshentsokhov.

When finally I was a civilian, I had two thousand Polish marks in my pocket as well as thirty-two cigarettes (three new ones, the rest crumpled and yellow, with four- and five-digit numbers on them), and a letter with the return address of one "Jakob Vizner, Custom Tailor" printed on the envelope.

That letter, without heading or preamble began, "I am writing to tell you . . ." It went on to say that my father was dead, and that his landlord had put new tenants into his two-room apartment on the third floor. At the close of the letter, Jakob Vizner added, "According to the rent control law, a dead tenant's son who is serving in the army retains rights to his father's apartment and is deemed to be a tenant himself." Folded inside the letter was a clipping from a Yiddish newspaper that read:

LEGAL ADVICE

Mr. Jakob Vizner: "If a father dies and his only son is serving in the army . . ."

Then followed the rest of Jakob Vizner's advice in the letter.

I racked my brain, but could not remember any Jakob Vizner in our old apartment building. Clearly he was some newcomer to our neighborhood who was prompted by a decent sympathy to write.

Thinking about my hometown, I realized that I had no one there who could be of any help to me. I had no relatives—indeed I knew nobody anymore. It was clear too that I would not be able to find work there. It seemed foolish, then, to go back merely to embroil myself in a quarrel with a landlord, especially since I did not need an apartment all for myself.

I had spent four years in the Polish army. For six months I served on the Bolshevik front. I spent five months in the Ukraine and in eastern Galicia. But as I was being discharged from the 27th Infantry Regiment in Tshentsokhov, I had no idea where I would go.

Three soldiers, newly released like myself from the army, stood before the ticket window of the 27th Regiment's travel office. One was a German from Pomerania; another was from Novo-Radomsk. The third soldier was from Lodz.

The German was the first to get his free travel voucher, then it was the turn of the Pole from Novo-Radomsk. The fellow just ahead of me was the soldier from Lodz. He was a tall man, angular, serious, and lean. A man with a broad face. The sort of man who, at Christian funerals, is always given the death lamp to carry.

The lean Pole, ecstatic because he was finally going home, stood smiling radiantly. The corners of his mouth were dimpled like the surface of a pond into which a frog has just dived. He spoke to no one.

"Where to?" came the voice of the lieutenant whose head showed behind the glass of the ticket booth.

"To Lodz," the tall lean Pole cried, and there was so much joy, so much human yearning in his voice that I felt its warmth streaming over me. The name of the town to which he was going sank like an anchor into my mind. When it was my turn at the ticket window and the head behind the glass asked, "Where to?" I stammered, "L . . . Lodz."

And that's how it was that I came to Lodz.

1

It was one of those days when the sun deceives everyone. The overcast sky was massed with fragmented clouds from which there fell a slow drizzle that had in it the smell of a moist, snow-tinged autumn. And then sunlight burst through the raindrops, serving to remind us that summer was not entirely gone. The municipal park was shrouded in a dark gray fog that seemed to be waiting for the quick rain to be gone so it could again envelop the pale birches. There was nobody on the intersecting paths beside which stood green chairs, now abandoned and strewn with withered yellow leaves.

I walked up and down the main path. One! Two! Left! Right! I marched, military fashion, with my eyes on the clock in the bell tower: I was making eight paces every ten seconds. Hurry up. Quickly. Quickly. It has to be ten paces every ten seconds. In his little hut that looked like the cabin of a ship, the watchman sent suspicious glances my way. The rain intensified.

"It's stupid to be drenched to the skin," I said, interrupting my military march. I raised the collar of my soldier's topcoat and walked quickly to the gleaming iron gates that seemed to have been polished by the rain.

Near the gate, the watchman sat in his hut and looked irritably out at me through slits in the planking. He had the almond-shaped eyes that pigs, and sometimes crows, have. It was clear that he had opinions about my sort. I knew exactly what he was thinking: "A soldier . . . not a soldier . . . the devil only knows what he is. Spends whole days wandering about in the park trying to figure out how to steal the shovels leaning against the hut. What else does a fellow like that have on his mind?"

I went quickly out into the street, avoiding his eyes, and strode over the wet asphalt with the same quick military pace I had used before.

It was nearly six o'clock in the evening. There were few people on the street. A man wearing glasses went by. A woman under a blue umbrella. And somebody else.

I walked about this way for something like half an hour. Then I noticed I was counting paces again with my eyes as well as in my head. This made me laugh. *So that's how it is. I'm still a soldier—to the very bone.*

When the marching fatigued me, I stopped at a street corner and asked myself, *What's your hurry?* I had no idea what the right answer was.

In the several weeks since I had been hanging about the town, I had become acquainted with—and made only too much use of—the places where one could hope to get in out of the rain, or where one might run into somebody one knew. In the waiting rooms of the town's two train stations I was already well known as a bad penny. To the women who kept the buffet counters and to the people at the newspaper kiosks I was a suspicious character. I did not leave those places because anyone threatened me in any way but because I felt myself overwhelmed by pity—by self-pity.

How could a healthy, vigorous person like me be down and out?

In those weeks of knocking about in Lodz, I had grown accustomed to the pathetic silence of my life. I felt my soul being swallowed up in the rhythms of idleness, of futility. There is something about wandering the strange streets of a large industrial city, trying to warm oneself by the light of a chilly sun, turning weaker and weaker with hunger—there is something in all this that separates, alienates one from the entire world.

I even learned to like my black, bitter loneliness and the constant yearning for food and a clean shirt. I learned to ignore people's sneers and to keep moving.

Just a couple of hours ago I met someone with whom I had served in the army. I stopped him.

He was a sly young man with shifty, tiny eyes no bigger than peas—eyes like a fox. I've no idea why I stopped him. He was wearing a well-pressed red suit and a visored cap. He had changed, put on weight, and I wondered how I had been able to recognize him.

"Bornshtayn," I called. He turned and gave me a hostile look. "Don't you recognize me?" I asked.

"No," he said, looking disdainfully at my sad clothing.

"I'm—"

"You served with me in the army?"

"Yes. That's me."

"What do you want?"

I considered what I ought to say. He had been the huckster, the peddler of our regiment. I remembered that he had trafficked in everything—bread, shoes, new confederation hats with tin visors which were not issued to every soldier. In his footlocker there was always what seemed an entire warehouse of hats, buttons for uniforms, underwear, white bread, cheese, sausage, and so on.

He did business everywhere, on the march, in the trenches, at the front, on the line. And since he was forbidden to have his footlocker with him at the front, he sold cigarettes. No matter how much I've thought about it since then, it's still beyond me how he found cigarettes. Soldiers, even officers and Red Cross nurses, came to his trench to buy the cigarettes he acquired on the firing line.

Had he been struck by a Bolshevik bullet, it might well have been said of him: "He wheeled and dealed with his last breath."

Thinking about Bornshtayn, one was tempted to add wheeling and dealing to the list of sports like football, horse racing, swimming, sailing, and so on. Bornshtayn loved to sell cigarettes at dangerous moments on the battlefield in the same way that a skillful ship's captain will risk his vessel in a storm.

"Well, Bornshtayn, how are you?" I asked.

"Not bad," he said, turning his head and making a move to go.

"Do you want to buy something from me?" I asked, not really knowing what I had to sell.

He quickly turned his sly, well-nourished head. "What have you got?"

"Just a minute, I'll get it."

I stepped into a doorway and took the belt off my trousers, then replaced it with a string. I had taken the broad yellow belt with its heavy brass buckle from a captured Ukrainian officer in Lemberg. I offered Bornshtayn the buckle, too.

He looked at my wares and frowned. "This stuff! I don't buy this sort of thing these days."

I felt desperate. "Bornshtayn, give me five hundred marks for the belt. It's worth three thousand."

I hadn't eaten all day, and I was beside myself at the thought that he would not buy the belt.

He walked on without looking back. In all of Lodz, that moment, he was the only person I knew. I could not bear to see him leave. I was overwhelmed just then by the sort of fellow feeling, the sort of intimacy that someone lost in a town feels when he comes upon somebody he knows.

"Bornshtayn," I said, "do you remember when I gave you half a chicken—free? Without charging you a cent? Do you remember? It was near Skalmerzhe, where the crucifix was chopped down." My voice trembled.

Near Minsk we had been in the same trench together for several days. Without food. Bornshtayn had groaned and wept. He had complained about being hungry and cursed his father for not having crippled him so he could avoid the Polish draft.

I found my way to a peasant's hut some thirty paces from our trench. The peasant gave me a loaf of bread and a roast chicken, half of which I brought back to Bornshtayn, who was lying half dead in the trench, his rifle pointed not at the enemy but at himself.

"Bornshtayn, do you remember? Do you remember? You were practically starving and I brought you half a chicken? Near where the crucifix was chopped down."

He kept walking as if he hadn't heard. Then he stopped, took several bills from his pocket, handed them to me, and started off again.

I took the money, then ran after him. I threw the buckled belt, as if it were a large bagel, over his head. Then I turned and ran off.

Bornshtayn, feeling the belt, cried out as if he felt a noose around his neck. He removed it quickly and shoved it into a pocket.

I bought half a loaf of bread in a bakery. Half of that I ate standing in a doorway. Half an hour later I was hungry again, and I devoured the rest of the bread.

The sunshine proved deceptive. Once again it rained, this time more heavily. My clothes were soaked, and my shoes filled with mud. I tried to think of someplace to go where I could be out of the rain. Standing in doorways was beginning to irk me.

I resumed my street wandering.

I stopped at Vidzhevska Street, as if wakened by the thin melody that floated out into the night from the small Russian church there.

I went inside. Some dozen people were kneeling before the altar, whispering their evening prayers. I removed my hat and also knelt.

The tenor music of the pious throng pulsated in the vaulted space, its echo hovering for several moments in the close air before it died away in the dark corners of the church.

Still kneeling, I dozed off. The singing seemed very far away.

I was wakened by the sound of a hoarse, deep voice. I looked about. Everyone else was standing respectfully watching my "devotions." I got quickly to my feet.

A priest who reminded me of King Barbarossa—his shaggy hair and his beard were so red—was delivering the sermon. He was saying that the Almighty had a particular affection for his children, the Russian Orthodox people. Meaning to test whether they were faithful to Him, the Lord had sent the Antichrist, the Bolsheviks—Trotsky. The Lord then united Himself to the Antichrist and thereby learned that his children, the Russian Orthodox people, were indeed unfaithful.

"Seeing this . . ." The priest groaned. There were tears in his eyes. "Seeing this, the Holy Spirit departed from the Russian Orthodox children and from their Mother Russia, and Heaven decreed that the Russian Orthodox people should spend seventy-five years in exile under the rule of the Antichrist—the Bolsheviks."

The priest's sermon was accompanied by sighs, by sorrowful murmurs. A couple of old women sobbed into their handkerchiefs and cried out at intervals, "Woe unto you, Mother Russia."

An old Russian general who had a sea of brass, silver, and gold medals on his chest beat his breast as he prayed, "Dear Christ, have pity on Russia."

When the priest's sermon was over, the congregation slowly dispersed, pausing first to kiss the priest's plump, almost swollen, hand. Outside it was still raining. For ten or fifteen minutes more I walked about in the streets. Then I went back to the house in which I lodged.

2

The cellar where I lived was long and narrow and always shrouded in dense shadow. The cubicles into which it was divided were long and narrow, like the corridor that led to them. There were seven small rooms there. Five of them were used as storage spaces, while a couple of families lived in the other two. The head of one of the households was a wagon driver who worked for the city carting off human waste; the head of the other was an old half-mad shoemaker.

I stayed in the shoemaker's home.

As I came into the corridor, I heard the fresh, sprightly laughter of children coming from the courtyard. The door to the shoemaker's cubicle was open. No one was inside. I went in and shut the door, wondering as I did so where the old man might be. Then I heard his hoarse voice in the corridor, "Give it to him . . . give it to him, Stockya." He was playing with the children.

A small lamp burned on the wall. A couple of straw mattresses lay flung together on the floor. There were potatoes cooking in a pot in the earthenware hearth, and dense clouds of steam hovered like smoke in the cellar.

Near the small window there stood a low table on which various implements of the shoemaker's art were scattered. Old shoes and scraps of shoes lay under the table. A three-legged cobbler's stool stood nearby. There was no other furniture in the room except for a second table, a wooden bench, and a ragged straw basket.

On the filthy walls from which dark green moisture oozed there hung a portrait of Jesus and Mary, as well as color pictures of Polish heroes clipped from magazines: Kościuszko, Poniatowski, Pilsudski, and others.

I was exhausted, wet clear through. I flung my coat off quickly, removed my shoes, and threw myself on one of the straw mattresses and covered myself with the ragged cotton quilt that lay there.

I couldn't fall asleep. The smell of the potatoes boiling roused my hunger. It was nearly two weeks since I had had any soup or a midday meal.

"King, O King, spare his life!" I heard the voices of children in the corridor and then the clatter of their running feet.

Whenever the old shoemaker had time, he played military games with the eight children in the house. It was when he talked about warfare that his madness was particularly noticeable. When he called out his commands, the half-cracked old man's mustaches arched proudly and his eyes glowed with a strange light. He stood ramrod straight and issued fiery orders. He was continually chanting, "March! March, Dombrowski!"

Now, followed by the children in formation, he goose-stepped into the cellar, his eyes blazing. The boys wore paper hats and carried wooden guns on their shoulders as they escorted the seven-year-old Fabianik, who had neither hat nor wooden gun.

Unaware of my presence, the old man seated himself ceremoniously on the three-legged cobbler's bench. The children formed a line before him and respectfully saluted.

A blond, hungry-looking boy with a gleaming potato face took two steps forward. "What shall we do, O King, with conquered Germany?" he said, stammering his rehearsed speech as he pointed to Fabianik, the little "prisoner" whom two children held firmly by his shoulders.

Fabianik, a weak child with slender, bowed legs, looked stunned, pale, and apathetic. His protruding, watery eyes wandered foolishly about the room like an idiot's.

The "king" rose from the cobbler's bench. "What shall we do with conquered Germany, dear soldiers?" he said heatedly. "We must once and for all draw his tigerish teeth; he must be destroyed once and for all." Ardent and serious, he stood with his head bowed. Then, raising a hand, he cried passionately, "In the name of Ourselves, King of the great Polish nation; in the name of the Polish nobility; in the name of the one and only God and His son the redeemer Jesus Christ, I condemn the conquered Kaiser of the German nation to death. Today must mark an end to the existence of the eternal enemy of Poland who has for thousands of years devoured the best of her children—the strongest sons of the holy Polish nation."

His scalding contempt, his wild movement, and the seriousness hidden in his words terrified the children, whose faces turned solemn and pale.

The little "prisoner," Fabianik, as if it had slowly reached him that *he* was the German Kaiser, began to tremble, and into his face there came a look of terrified helplessness.

As a matter of fact, Fabianik was German.

His mother, Stepha, had lived with a German noncommissioned officer during the occupation of Poland, and it was he who had fathered the boy.

The poor child was hated by everyone. But he was most particularly detested by the old shoemaker.

Fabianik, a weak child with a narrow chest and a large round head perched on a long slender neck, was the butt of the children's most casual anger. They cursed him, tormented him and beat him. It was a dreadful sight to see the children or the old man mauling him with hands, fists, belts, sticks—anything within reach. Always he was called the Schwab—the Swabian—rather than Fabianik. If something was lost, it was the Schwab who had taken it. If something was broken, it was the Schwab who had done it. By the time he was three Fabianik had learned not to cry, as if he understood that tears would do him no good. Child though he was, he accepted that it was his destiny to be beaten, cursed, and tormented for no better reason than that he was a Schwab, a German. The boy endured silently and calmly the blows that came his way and though his eyes might plead for compassion, there was never a trace—not so much as a gleam—of a single tear in them.

Because the children were ashamed to play with him, he acquired the habit of being alone. Isolated from them all, he had his secret dark corners where he made dolls out of bits of dough, where he kneaded animals and people out of clay. If the children intruded on his hiding places and disturbed him or stole his nests of animals, he pretended to ignore them and, without scowling, went quietly off to find some other hiding place where he began again to collect dough and clay with which to make his collection of lions, horses, people, and cats. Not the slightest trace of pain or sorrow in his dull, immobile face; in his soul every impulse of protest, of resistance against torment, had been uprooted.

I had had occasion to notice that Fabianik avoided sunlight. He was drawn to the dark. To shadows. To whatever was veiled and obscure. He avoided the clear light of day, as if he feared he might be noticed—seen. And Fabianik was not supposed to be seen. Was supposed to keep his distance. Because he was a Schwab.

So he was drawn to darkness and shadows, and things of the night, and concealment. There was no touch of the sun on his features, no trace of daylight, of brightness.

He was, in short, a sort of human worm who was always to be found in dark corners, in hidden nooks and crannies.

As I lay on the straw pallet, I was curious to see what was going to happen to the child.

Into the old man's increasingly wild and feverish eyes there came now a venomous glow of hatred—that eternal hatred of the Germans against whom, at every opportunity, he pronounced maledictions.

"They've ruined our homeland," he cried with mounting excitement, his voice hoarse, exalted. "The holy country that Christ blessed with wealth and excellence. They have driven our queen Wanda into the waves of the Vistula. They have hounded us for centuries, thinking eternally of ways to exterminate us. To wipe us from the face of the earth. They sent the devil Martin Luther into Christ's world in order to poison pure Christian belief. Lord"—in the grip of his mounting excitement, he was suddenly on his knees before the holy picture—"I will praise Thy name in all the corners of the earth for that Thou hast delivered mine enemy into my hand. Wherever I encounter the light of Thy day, there shall I utter my prayers to you." His palms pressed together, he spoke with the passionate, exalted voice of a mystic.

The children "soldiers" stood rooted where they were, embarrassed and frightened, their eyes fixed on the old man, their mouths open, their fearful hearts beating frantically.

The two boys who were holding the "Kaiser" by his shoulders dug their fingers more firmly and deeper into his flesh. Fabianik, who was wearing only a ragged and filthy little shirt and a pair of torn shorts tied with a bit of twine, knew now what was going to happen. He turned pale as a corpse, and rigid with terror. His lips formed a grimace, his eyes protruded even farther than usual from their sockets, and his teeth began to chatter.

Moving swiftly, the old man got up from his knees. With the lightness of a cat he leaped to the frayed basket from which he took a white sheet and a length of clothesline. With nails and a hammer he tacked the sheet to the wall, then tied one end of the rope to an overhead water pipe and made a noose with the other.

"But it's appalling. He really means to hang the child," I said, but no one heard me.

His face was suffused with blood. Gritting his teeth, the old man cried, "Give him to me!" And woe to any of the boys who might have thought to disobey him.

I lay paralyzed, unable to think what to do.

The boys led the "Kaiser" up to the old man. Fabianik twitched and looked hopelessly at the clothesline, at the sheet on the wall, at the shoemaker's inflamed, unfocused eyes. The boy's chin quivered; a pair of folds, signs of his despair, appeared in the corners of his mouth. He knew that the clothesline was meant to hang him, but he did not understand what was the dreadful sin he had committed to deserve so dire a punishment.

The dark red glow from the hanging lamp cast an aura around the shoemaker's face. In the oppressive silence in which one could clearly hear the beating of the children's hearts there pulsed the expectation of some dreadful event. That ominous feeling was both heightened and shadowed by the usual dreariness that haunts any cellar that supports the weight of three stories of stone and concrete, plaster and wood, people and steel.

The children regarded the old man with shocked, staring eyes that were attentive to the least gesture of his hand or finger, to every movement of his blood-suffused and hate-filled face, and to every thought that half manifested itself in his expression or in the fragmented words that escaped him.

Tick, tock. Into the anguished silence there intruded the sound of a clock in the story above the cellar.

Suddenly Fabianik tore himself loose from his captors, flung himself to the floor, and beat his large, wispy-haired blond head against the stones, screeching wildly like a calf that has escaped the slaughterer's knife with its throat half cut. His shriek had sheer animal terror in it, mingled with a passionate and profoundly soulful human fear of death. It was an uncanny sound, a quavering childlike prayer for pity and for life.

The cry only served to stir the old man's hate-poisoned blood. His sparse, dingy hair, like gray moss, stood on end; the line formed by his mustaches turned as angular and sharp as the tails of a couple of mice. The nostrils of his red nose flared as if he meant to spurt fire through them. Opening wide his twisted mouth, he turned toward Fabianik, who continued to whimper and to beat his head against the stone floor, and burst into wild, convulsive, asthmatic laughter. "Ha, ha, ha! Hee, hee, hee. So . . . so that's the way . . . that's the way Kaiser Wilhelm the Second dies. Kha . . . kha . . ."

Here he began to cough, "Agh! Agh! You shame those of your

ancestors who besieged Julius Caesar's mighty Roman Empire." He bent nearly double over the diminutive Fabianik, who lay on the ground howling like a dog.

"So, Excellency. So, German Kaiser and King of Prussia, would you care to sing?

Deutschland, Deutschland über alles,
Über alles in der Welt!

He sang mockingly, mispronouncing the German words, interrupting himself frequently to cough, wheeze, giggle, or snort. All at once he grew weary. Straightening himself up, he called, "Marshal Foch."

There was no reply. The children seemed no longer to know what world they inhabited. They stood in place as if carved out of stone, or as if they were immobile dolls with whom the mad old man played.

I lay on my straw ticking, stunned, paralyzed with fear. Could he really mean to hang the boy?

It was the devil himself who stood before me, enclosed in an armor of hatred and flame.

Casting a scornful glance at the children he said, "Marshal Foch," in the menacing, contemptuous tone of a colonel or a general.

At the second command, a small round-faced boy with a pointed chin, a narrow forehead, and the look of a hungry mouse stepped forward. He made a well-rehearsed bow and said, "At your orders, Your Majesty."

The old man responded to the greeting with a crooked smile that revealed his yellow, decaying, "royal" teeth. Then he called again, "Marshal Josef Pilsudski, Commander-in-Chief of the Polish army!"

Another boy with a complexion as green as an unripe fall apple stepped forward and bowed. "At your orders, Your Gracious Highness."

Again the old man straightened up. He lifted his head, coughed, then said in an elevated tone, "I hereby grant to General Foch and to Marshal Pilsudski the honor of leading Wilhelm Hohenzollern, Emperor of Germany and King of Prussia, to his execution." The two "generals" were so frightened they could hardly stand.

A sardonic smile appeared on the old man's wrinkled face, giving it the look of a ghostly mask.

Addressing "Marshal Foch," the old man went on: "I understand that in your country the guillotine, your nation's pride, is preferred in such matters. But in my view it would be a sin against God and France to use the instrument that lopped the head off the noble Louis XVI to decapitate Wilhelm II, whose crimes are on a par with those of common highwaymen or pirates. A rope is sufficient for him."

"Marshal Foch," whose knees trembled, and who understood nothing of what the old man said, stood sucking his thumb. "Pilsudski," taut as a fiddle string, was so scared that he heard nothing at all. The other boys, as if transformed by a necromancer's curse, seemed frozen where they stood.

The old man seemed to glow with the heat of madness, as if his soul, like the wick in a lamp, were blazing in his body. "Bring the Kaiser here," he commanded brusquely.

"Pilsudski" and "Foch" went to Fabianik and bent over him. Touching his shoulders carefully, lightly, they said gently, "Get up. Get up."

Fabianik turned his raw stupid gaze on the two boys. Though there was no trace of a tear in his eyes, his mouth was distorted, as if by some profound strange pain. There was a thin dirty white spume on his compressed lips. He lifted his head and looked about him with the disordered look of a calf that has received the butcher's first stunning blow.

The eyes of both "Marshal Foch" and "Josef Pilsudski" filled with tears. "Spare him, Grandpa," they cried. "Spare him."

The shoemaker turned ferociously on them. The word "Grandpa" had shattered his bright imagined world of royalty and beauty, and he was back in his hateful abyss of poverty and need. No throne, no power, no wealth. The word "Grandpa" had wakened him; had wreaked havoc with the throne of his dreams.

Stamping his feet and tearing at his hair, he cried, "Whose grandfather do you take me for, eh? Your grandfather is an old shoemaker, a nobody, a nothing. He's a drunkard whom poverty and heartache, sorrow and pain killed long ago. Hindenburg's soldiers turned his daughter into a street woman, a whore. Your grandfather lies buried under a fence because all his life he was a filthy ass who could never live like a decent Christian; who in a damp cellar drove his tuberculous wife into her grave—and all for want of a bit of milk.

"No, no. I'm no grandfather of yours—I'm the King of Poland. Respect! Do you hear? Honor me! Salute! Tremble! Fall on your knees, because with a single word I can have you torn to bits—you devils, you scoundrels, regicides, perjurors . . . *canaille*."

The old man's fury made him foam at the mouth. He stamped his feet; he gritted his teeth. His hands were balled into fists; in his frenzy his arms seemed ready to leap from their sockets.

His contorted face, now a blue-tinged red, looked like a warped mask, a mask in which the nose, mouth and eyes were not in their proper places—were jumbled together to express an insane, inhuman wrath.

Then he leapt like a wolf and, with one trembling hand, seized the rope hanging from the pipe as with the other he gripped Fabianik.

I could stand it no longer.

I jumped to my feet and with every ounce of my strength punched the old man in the chest. As if he had been poleaxed, he fell to the floor, his arms out-flung. From his bony withered chest there came the sound of wheezing groans.

The children set up a mounting wail. For a moment or two the old man lay inert, showing no signs of life. Through his parched lips a foamy spittle oozed. He lay entirely still except for the twitching of the little finger of his right hand.

I stood like someone who had entirely lost his reason. I looked first at the terrified weeping children and then at the old man. He opened his eyes and looked up at me. Never in all my days have I seen such eyes in a human face. His crossed eyeballs protruded from their sockets. They were framed with a thin dark line of dirty blood. The lower eyelashes of his left eye were gummed against the eyeball and gave off a glitter that appeared on the upturned eye like tiny, hardly perceptible dots.

"Satan! Antichrist! Assassin!" he shouted wildly, spewing out the words as if he had to move them swiftly to make room for the unuttered curses that were still hidden in his heart or on his tongue.

I put on my soldier's topcoat and left the house accompanied on my way by the old man's yells and the cries of the children.

As I came up into the courtyard, I heard the swift drumming of feet. The children were making their escape.

The worst consequence of the "Polish King" episode was that I was once again without a place to sleep. It was impossible to return to my bed in the old man's house. His insane pride would not have permitted the presence in his house of one who had struck him, and particularly, if he should learn that I was a Jew.

The rain had stopped falling. A sharp, near winter breeze was blowing from the southern part of town, drying the pavement and the asphalt of the sidewalks.

I started off and felt something tickling my right arm. At first, thinking someone was accosting me, I looked around, but what I saw turned out to be simple enough: a yellow patch from the worn sleeve of my military overcoat had peeled away, providing the wind easy access to my stiff, coarsely sewn canvas shirt.

I wondered, "*Now, how did I get a new tear?*" In the last few days my bare flesh showed through more and more rents in my coat, like open wounds in a diseased body.

It was just like me to stand there for a considerable while wondering what had hooked my coat and torn it. I tormented myself trying to remember each place I had been that day and the day before, but I could not recall where or how the coat could have been torn. Sadly I concluded that the rents on the coat signified a new visitation in my unfortunate life. That I was being dogged step-by-step, and that even my overcoat was being tormented.

It was cold, and the only remedy against it was to enter into a long dialogue with myself. For hours on end my thoughts about heaven only knows what sort of foolish matters kept me from feeling the cold, and from acknowledging that winter was really and truly here.

I had to laugh at the strange sly tricks a person can play to outwit the cold hands and freezing body that yearn for warmth in a bed.

I walked the streets for several hours until it was gate-locking time. I could hear on all sides the hoarse groan of rusted keys turning in the locks of great iron gates.

How strange.

It seemed to me that *I* was being locked up in a lonely, foreign street in which I would never find a warm place to spend the night.

In the more than four years since I had been drafted I hadn't once felt the soft caress of a woolen comforter.

The ringing of the keys made a poisonous, hateful sound in my ears. I had been locked inside a street. No matter where I went, it would be one street after another.

Where could I find lodging for the night? If I had three hundred marks, I could go to the house of the little Jew near the train station where I had spent several nights following my discharge, when I still had some money.

The cold was creeping into my bones. On top of everything else, I was still suffering from a light fever and from the excitement of the "Polish King" episode. I shivered, and it seemed to me that my scalp was tingling.

Where to find three hundred marks? It was dark, and the wind tossed the branches of the trees.

You've had it, I said to myself. *No amount of twisting and turning will do you any good. You're going to die in the street.*

I discerned a shadow ahead of me on the otherwise empty street. I ran toward it, feeling an uncanny joy, as if I was expecting the arrival of a good friend.

It was a middle-aged woman. She wore a broad-brimmed, dark hat that hid her features. She carried a woven basket in her right hand.

"Good evening, ma'am," I said.

She did not reply. It was clear that I had frightened her. She stood open-mouthed, regarding me with suspicion.

"What a heavy load you're carrying. It's too heavy for a woman," I said, hardly aware of my words as I took the woven basket from her. She uttered a ragged cry, turned, and ran away, leaving me holding the basket. Stunned, I stood for a while beside the wall. "I'm being taken for a thief . . . God knows I don't look very respectable," I said, and started briskly off after her, meaning to pursue her. "Ma'am . . . excuse me, ma'am," I called as loudly as I could so that the frightened woman, who was already some distance away, could hear me. "Excuse me, ma'am. But I'm no thief. I'm no crook. Here, take back your basket."

"Oh, no you don't. You want to steal the few gulden I own. Help! Police!" she cried, panic-stricken.

I looked around in both directions, but there was no one to be seen—anywhere. "I swear, lady . . . I swear by all I hold dear . . . Really, I'm not going to rob you."

"I know your type. Oh, I know. Rascals. Don't stand there pretending to be a respectable citizen. You want to rob me." And with that, she was off again, running.

It took only a few quick military strides before I caught up with her.

With some violence, I shoved the basket into her hands, turned, and went back the way I had come.

When I was some yards away, she stopped, turned, then thought for a while, after which she called, "You, young fellow. Come back here. Come on back."

I turned. She watched me intently, studying my face through the blue lenses of the glasses which at first I had not noticed because they were obscured by the wide brim of the hat she had pulled low on her head. Then, opening her reticule, she took out a bank note and pushed it into my hand. "Take it. Take it, young man. You seem to be a soldier, eh? You were a soldier. You'll have to excuse me for thinking you might be a thief. You really are very badly dressed. And your face looks awful. And on top of that it's night and the street is so quiet and badly lighted. Oh, to hell with the new Prime Minister. He keeps inventing new wars, and young soldiers die of hunger." She spoke hastily, spurting words. Fear still lingered in her face. "Is it true? You aren't really a thief, are you? I shouldn't wonder if you were. You have the look of a man who hasn't had anything to eat in three days. To hell with the new Prime Minister—you look like death warmed over. Like a skinned chicken that was sick before it was slaughtered. That's how you look. You need to rest. You could get consumption—there's no curing that disease. To hell with the new Prime Minister."

Her body and her hands were in constant motion, and her speech was garbled, though from time to time the sentence "To hell with the new Prime Minister" rose like a curse out of its flow.

Finally, having convinced herself that I was not a thief, she gave me a benign look and handed me her basket to carry.

"I understand, young man. You don't want to be given money for doing nothing. It was very good of you not to kill me. Nice that you haven't become a crook. On the other hand, what good would it have done you to kill me? All I have in the world is a thousand marks. My shoes are worth five thousand. The laundry in the basket, my blouse, my skirt, my stockings, and my hat—another five thousand marks. The cheese and butter that I got from my father-in-law in the country, four thousand marks. Altogether some twenty-four thousand marks. You know, for stealing twenty thousand marks one can be condemned by a state court to a firing squad."

Her prattle made me laugh, but my mirth puzzled her. She peered at me through her lenses and wiggled her snub nose. "You don't believe me, young man? You laugh. Come home with me and I'll show you a copy of the *Courier*, August 18. There's a whole page there describing how one Michael Kvitshik from the village of Shniadev stole thirteen thousand marks from the villager Antoni Stshuparek. A state court in Plotsk condemned Shniadev to the firing squad. And they actually shot him. For stealing no more than thirteen thousand marks."

All at once she looked as if she was about to cry. "Ah . . . ah," she sighed. "Young people. Children, still at their mother's breast— eighteen-year-olds rounded up and thrown into battle—there they learn to kill people, to shoot, to slaughter each other. And they come back and God is gone from their hearts; they are wild, undisciplined, ruined—wandering about in the streets like birds of prey, ready to twist someone's head off or cut their throats for a thousand marks. Every day there are red placards on the wall announcing: 'Condemned . . . State Court . . . Death penalty . . . Procurator Schmidt.' To hell with the new prime minister. A pity. A pity. They're such children.

"Young man," she said, changing her tone abruptly, "you've no idea how grateful I am to you because you haven't turned into a crook." Her pale, maternal features glowed with pleasure and contentment. She beamed at me as if I had done her some very great service. All her fear was gone, and she looked like a genial, slightly bewildered woman.

She stopped before a house with a high wall. "Here's where I live," she said. I handed her the basket. Again, she pressed a bit of paper into my hand. I took it silently. It occurred to me to ask her for a place to sleep.

"Perhaps, ma'am, you could put me up for the night? I'll be glad to sleep on the bare ground. My bones are used to it," I said, with forced sprightliness. "They learned to put up with it during the war."

She sighed and shook her head. "No, young man. My children, my husband, and I live in a single room. The porter of the house hates us. Tomorrow morning he would be sure to announce to the whole courtyard that Madame Voitshikov entertains soldiers at night. No, I can't do it. No."

She opened her purse once more, took out another bill, and handed it to me. "Take it. Take it, young man. It'll help you to a bed. Just keep your courage up. You'll survive until you get a chance to earn some money of your own. A young fellow like you isn't going to be lost. We don't live among wolves."

She took my hand and held it, saying almost tearfully, "Goodbye, young fellow. Try not to make a wrong turn. Things won't always be as bad as they are now. Goodbye. If you need help, come to me. This is where I live, on the third floor. There, you see the little window with the green curtain." She pointed toward it. "I've never turned a needy person away. *Adieu*, my friend. Don't forget—come back and visit me."

I was touched by her courtesy and answered her with a warm handshake. I could feel my rigid loneliness dissolving. "Dear lady, thank you. Thank you."

"Wait a bit. I'm going to throw something down to you from my window," she called as she went inside. "You can give it back to me someday."

The sleepy porter, wearing a white sheepskin coat whose high collar entirely framed his head, peered out and opened the gate.

A little while later a window on the third floor opened—the window with the green curtain—and a head appeared. The head of the woman with the blue eyeglasses.

"Watch out," she called and threw a newspaper-wrapped package down to me.

"*Adieu*." The word mixed with a sigh could just be heard. Then the window closed. In the package there were cheese, butter, and bread wrapped in broad green leaves that still had the smell of a country village in them.

With the package tucked under my arm, I started off to find a lodging for the night.

All at once I became aware that I was near the shoemaker's house. The gate was open. The porter had forgotten to close it.

"Yes. I'll go in and see how the old fellow is. Who knows, I may have killed him." I moved quickly through the courtyard. Near the cellar, I paused. Silently, carefully, I bent down to the little window.

The old man was alone in the large room. He was kneeling rigidly, as if congealed, before the picture of Jesus and Mary.

I was assailed by a sharp pang of anxiety. What if he was bidding farewell to his own life? Perhaps I had struck his chest too hard with my fist. Why had I interfered? He was mad, or anyhow, half mad. I could have handled the matter in some harmless fashion. It was simple enough: I could have driven the children from the cellar and taken the rope away from him.

Five or six minutes passed and still the old man knelt before the holy picture. Perhaps he had died in that rigid posture. I had heard that one could die while in a cataleptic state. Why such long prayers at night? In all the time I had stayed with him I had never seen him praying at such great length.

Then he stood up, rubbed his hands, and went over to his little stove. He panted, and as he stood over the stove the steam made him cough. He wiped his mustache, then took a rag with which he removed a pot of boiling potatoes from the stove. He poured off the water, then laid the potatoes out on a metal platter.

"Thank God, he's alive," I whispered, relieved.

From some drawer or other the old man produced a herring, then sat down at the table and began to eat, moving his mouth with its yellow teeth with such ecstasy that I was compelled to laugh.

"Yes. I'll go into the cellar."

I knocked at the door, but without waiting for a reply I opened it quickly and stood on the threshold.

Seeing me, the old man made a strangely twisted and fearful face.

Then he remembered me, and, his voice unnaturally high, he shouted, "Out, assassin. Get out, Communist. Gypsy! Out."

I tried to say something, but I could see that I had lost any chance I might have had to sleep in his house. I didn't brood over the fact but turned and, leaving the cellar, found my way back into the street.

There I opened the package the woman had given me and flung myself like a locust on the food it contained. In a matter of minutes I had gulped down all the bread and butter. At last I was full. Completely full. Then suddenly I felt a profound weariness—particularly a heaviness in my knees—as if lead had been poured all over my legs. I dragged myself about in the empty back streets for another half hour until I found myself before the Russian Orthodox church. I sat down on the top step and leaned my shoulders against one of the marble pillars that held up the vaulted ceiling of the front entryway.

For a moment or two my eyes took in the red brick wall of the building opposite me and saw how it pressed against a blue, half-dark, forbidding sky. A while later I saw nothing at all. As I fell asleep, it seemed to me that I was sitting on an iceberg and that my feet were encased in two floes of ice.

When I opened my eyes it was nearly dawn. There was no way to know the source of the billows of light that streaked the air only to be lost in the blue of the night that still encompassed the town.

The usual city birds were there. They sprang about on their thin legs on the massive church pillars and on the marble steps. Well rested and merry, they tilted their heads and, as if I were a newly arrived guest, regarded me with their small, sharp eyes.

Not far away a window was hastily opened and there appeared a blond, disheveled, nineteen-year-old woman, a sleepy look on her face, her ripe, half-naked breasts exposed.

She stood for a while and bathed her upper body in the cold early morning air, then she slammed the window shut. Presumably this was her way of testing the day's weather.

After an interval the door of a round vaulted balcony with a nickel balustrade opened. A man of some fifty years, a chair in his hand, came out on the balcony and sat down. The gigantic lungs inside his massive chest heaved with asthma as he coughed violently. His eyes were fixed, lifeless, as if they had been screwed into his face. Each time he uttered a racking cough he shook his head sharply, as if he meant to fling it from his shoulders, thereby ridding himself of his asthma once and for all.

The echo of his cough was harsh and resonant, like the echo of vibrating telephone wires in the street. His chest was red, thick, and wrinkled as a walnut. When he coughed, he clutched at his throat as if he were tearing at a rope that was choking off his breath.

On the other balcony there sat a man with a small, trimmed beard. He had a reddish gray bathrobe over his shoulders and wore soft yellow slippers of good-quality Moroccan leather. The bathrobe, one could easily tell, was old—perhaps from a time even before his marriage—because the robe failed to cover his chest or his expansive belly. It must have taken many years for him to acquire so much weight. He coughed quietly, steadily, without interruption.

"*Guten Tag, Herr Fischer,*" the man on the first-floor balcony called to him in German.

"*Guten Tag, Herr M.,*" the other man replied, taking out a box of pills. "The asthma drives me out of bed."

"Yes. It's dreadful."

"Do you use Penguin pastilles?"

"Yes, but they don't help. They're not the same as they were before the war. They're wartime ersatz. More than twenty years since I've been taking them, Herr M.," he said, half in German, half in Yiddish.

"Worthless goods. Worse than nothing. I threw them away. Before the war, they were real."

"*Ja, Herr Fischer.*"

As both men discussed their coughs, they began simultaneously and violently to cough. They groaned and sighed and shook their heads dolefully.

"*Ja, Herr M.*"

"*Ja, Herr Fischer.*"

The day was getting brighter. The fragmented clouds, wandering about in the sky as if they were both late and lost, were burned away as the newly arrived sun broke a bright way for itself out of the east. I was turning numb with the cold. I got up and moved off quickly in order to warm myself. Here and there night porters appeared, sweeping the streets. Battalions of workers, stretching and yawning sleepily, went silently into the factories, carrying blue coffee jugs under their arms.

4

There were several poorly clad people sitting on the broad benches that lined the long *allée* in the park. Near one of the benches a small crowd of workers and recently discharged soldiers was gathered. There was a lively discussion going on in which everyone took part. I watched the crowd for a while and listened, trying to figure out what the conversation was about.

One of the men, a slender fellow with bright eyes and thick unruly hair that fell over his thin, suntanned face, spoke angrily, gritting his teeth. "You shouldn't go. They put the foreign workers into barracks. They treat them like prisoners. Those French face-powder capitalists."

A good-humored older man with a light complexion and a thin blond mustache said, "That's a lie. I've just had a letter from my brother in France. He's not far from Verdun. He works nine hours, then he drinks wine and, for a groschen, gets to sleep with French women."

Everyone laughed.

"Yes," the dark man, still angry, said. "France provides the whole world with cosmetics, wine, and whores. If you go into one of our local nightclubs, the Ka-kardu, for instance, all you'll find is loose French women. To our women the French are all heroes, all Don Juans, as they are called. But the French don't like working. They sleep until noon, then breakfast on old sardines and sour Bordeaux wine. They regard our kind of workers as no better than African Negroes. 'Work, work, for as long as you have strength; that's what you were created for and nothing else. You're not French.' And should you complain because you're being housed in barracks surrounded by mud, the Frenchman scowls and says, 'That's no way to talk. It's impudent of you to say such things about France.' "

A third fellow, a calm, soft-spoken fellow, cut in, saying, "It's not true that there are French women in our local whorehouses. No. The loose ladies of Lodz learn a little French and claim to come from Paris. It's a trick to confuse the customers so they can raise their prices."

"Ah, what difference does it make?" interrupted another man whose famished voice expressed a longing for a good meal. "Polish, French, German, Jew—all of the bourgeoisie suck the marrow from our bones. Then, when we're at the very end of our strength, they invite us, along with our wives and children, to beat our heads against a wall. I don't expect to hit a jackpot. I'm going to sign up. Who's smart enough to know whether things there will go well or not? To hell with all whores: German, French—even our own. The point is to earn a little money and to have a decent place to sleep." He turned as if ready to go. "Well, fellows, who's going to sign up?"

Almost all of the men got to their feet and started off, talking and gesticulating. What I gathered from the discussion was that a group of French recruiters had come to town to sign men up for construction work in the devastated sections of northern France.

Excited and anxious, I followed the others. There was hope after all that my troubles might soon be over.

5

A crowd of some two hundred men stood near the entrance to a red factory. Above them, a sign read: WANTED, WORKERS FOR NORTHERN FRANCE.

The factory windows were grated with rusty iron bars behind which one could see cracked and smashed windowpanes.

A couple of hours went by before it was my turn to go in. In the main room, a small plump fellow who had the look of a businessman sat at a desk and regarded everyone and everything with a dry, cold look, as if everything he saw was merchandise he was about to buy. His plump chin almost touched his chest—it was almost as if he had no neck. In his short, stubby fingers he held a quill pen with which he wrote on a long sheet of paper.

Since I had no passport, he transcribed my name and age from my demobilization book, whose pages he turned over several times, as if searching for something. Finally, he said, "Your address isn't in here."

It was true. I had nearly forgotten that I didn't live anyplace. Without hesitation I gave him the shoemaker's address.

"Do you have a trade?" he asked, studying my papers with watery eyes that glistened as brightly as his oxfords—as if eyes and shoes had been treated with the same polish.

"No," I replied, unwilling to tell him that I had once kept the books of a corporation that no longer existed. I had heard it said that the French shied away from anyone who had been a bookkeeper, a correspondent, or the like.

Done with his questions, he raised a pudgy hand and pointed to the right. A narrow corridor led from the large room we were in to another, smaller room with a high, vaulted ceiling. As I passed down the corridor, I had the feeling I was in the gullet of the building. Old, thickly encrusted mold and spiderwebs seemed to look down from the ceilings and walls. And the high windows, with their smashed or cracked panes, gave the old factory the look of some huge dead hairy beast.

In the other room some twenty naked men stood shivering with cold. The wind blew in through the holes in the windows, stirring in their hair as through withered autumn leaves. The men were quiet, looking impatiently toward the door. Occasionally somebody muttered, "How long are they going to let us stand around naked like this?"

The blond fellow with the small mustache who had come with me from the park smoked his cigarette and made a joke: "The Frenchies must think we're Parisian women—why else would they keep us standing here naked?" Only three or four of the men laughed. There was not so much as a smile from any of the others; they shivered and kept still.

Some ten minutes later the doctor came in—a tall, heavy fellow with a massive flat-topped head on which there was not so much as a single hair to be seen. The thought came to me that one could set an inkwell on that flat head of his and write a letter there as easily as on a smooth table. There was a strange lassitude in his heavy careless gait. It resembled the stagger of a man still drunk with sleep. The instant I saw him I guessed that here was someone who, because he slept till noon, had never in twenty years seen a sunrise. I remembered what the dark angry worker had said about the French.

His entire face—composed mostly of deep wrinkles into whose midst there had somehow wandered eyes, a thick nose, a wide mouth with full sensual lips—spoke of the pleasures of the table: of roasted or pickled meats devoured in the late hours of the night.

Squinting with one eye, he studied us through a monocle, examining each of us, feeling our muscles with his fingers, turning us from one side to the other the way poor women turn meat in the butcher stalls of a market.

When he turned away from me I could feel the touch of his five sweaty fingers on my shoulders.

A little while later he was done with us. We got dressed and returned to the large room, where we waited.

Out of that whole crowd of men, only three were rejected. I was one of the three.

I felt hurt—mortified. Every hope I had had to climb out of my grave was shattered. I was so distressed that my hands trembled as I thought about once again having to resume my wandering through the streets, which had so discouraged me. I was dismayed at the prospect of having to scrabble again for a bit of food, for a place to sleep. Tears came to my eyes—tears of futility, of helplessness because I would be unable to rid myself of the stiff, vermin-ridden shirt that enclosed my body as in a case of armor. I was enraged because with this latest denial I had been given the message that I stood lower on the human scale than any of that ordinary crowd of hungry, unemployed drudges; that I had no place in God's great world; and that despite my entire willingness, my readiness to do any sort of work—despite all that, I was still superfluous.

6

I felt better in the street.

The bored midday sun, suspended in a gray sky, played with its weak, pale gold beams, sending them to shatter into prismatic jagged fragments in the windowpanes of houses.

A small old man stood before a notions shop warming his back in the sun. A little girl went by. Her attractive blond hair was combed back and braided into pigtails that were tied with red ribbons. Her features were as bright and clear as spring water. She was repeating a melody which had evidently been assigned to her by her teacher.

Suddenly she dropped a book from the bundle of notebooks and texts she carried under her arm.

I bent, picked up the fallen book, and handed it to her.

"Thank you," she said, her voice fresh, ringing. Then she went on.

I stood for a moment, like one surprised. The words "Thank you" stayed in my mind as something very important. The fresh ringing voice with which she had spoken them sounded for a while longer in my ears. She was already some distance down the street, but I could still see the gleam of her red ribbons and the motion of her golden hair, still hear the way she had said "Thank you."

Dear God, how long has it been since anyone spoke so simply to me? With wonder and with quiet sadness I made a quick calculation and concluded that not in years—not since I had been inducted into the army—had anyone spoken to me in that ordinary, human way. "Thank you." It was a phrase heard on every side, and yet, for the first time in weeks—perhaps in months—I felt simply delighted. It intoxicated me like wine. I felt marvelous. A sense of ease surged through my whole body.

I put my hand into my pocket and took out my last three thousand marks—the money the woman had given me—and hurried after the girl. Let the dear child buy herself some chocolate.

The city, the houses, the streets, the people—everything I looked at seemed stranger and more distant than before. I myself seemed smaller, lonelier, and more pitiful.

I was reminded of something that had happened to me when I was a boy of twelve.

7

I was playing with some children in the village marketplace when I fell under a peasant's wagon and badly bruised my right arm and hand.

At first my mother applied compresses to my hand, as well as some sort of dark salve that the barber-surgeon prescribed. I felt absolutely no pain.

But later the injured hand turned a bloodless pale green color, and the barber-surgeon advised my mother to take me to a doctor in the district capital. Otherwise there was danger that I could lose my hand.

My mother pawned the silver sabbath candlesticks and her silk shawl, which, as she had told us, had been a wedding present from her grandmother. She took several rubles, bundled me into an old sheepskin coat, got us aboard the train, and we were off to the city.

It was the first time in my life I had ever been to such a large place.

As the train approached the town, thousands of electric lights blazed up before me like eternally watchful flames. I had to close my eyes.

When I stuck my head out of the train window I could feel the play of the gas and electric lights dancing on my head and neck.

The locomotive began a hoarse, choked whistling.

In our town there was an asthmatic dog that hung about the marketplace. When the dog coughed, he too wheezed and whistled in the same hoarse, choked way as the locomotive.

With my eyes closed it seemed to me that all the cars of the train were being pulled by such a huge, huge dog. The dark, coal-smudged firemen were beating him with whips, compelling him to pull. Driving him on. Then I heard my mother's cry, "Child, get away from that window." She yanked me back to my place.

I had entirely forgotten that I was traveling to see a doctor and that there was a possibility that I might lose my hand. The train; the hours of rocking back and forth on the seat; the strange new people dressed in a variety of multicolored clothes; the unfamiliar woods and fields sown here and there with windmills and sawmills; the rivers that gleamed like mirrors before which the sun, the moon, the stars preened as they got ready to appear before people; the lamps, the streets, the stores, the shop windows—they all made me giddy and tired my eyes, which, with tenacious curiosity, tried to grasp and hold everything, everything. I was eager to seize on the most trivial sights in order to have something to tell my friends back home.

My mother pulled me along by the hand, repeating every few minutes, "Why don't you watch where you're going? You're running people down."

We stopped before a four-story building decorated with stucco and plaster cornices. My mother made inquiries of a passerby who nodded yes, and we ascended some brightly lighted marble stairs that were overlaid with linoleum. We stopped before a glass door. My mother pressed a button. We heard steps approaching, and the door opened.

A blond woman led us into a spacious room furnished with overstuffed velvet chairs. Almost at once there entered a tall, stout, freshly shaven man with a pimpled red nose. He looked very much like our town's community scribe, *Pan* Gidzhial, who every Sunday and every holiday used to get good and drunk, after which he put on a skirt and blouse and dropped in to Isaac the warder's house, where he chatted in broken Yiddish: "*Mazel top*, Isaac. They're going to eat a wedding canopy. I'm going to merry [sic] a good Jew."

Seeing the doctor, my mother stood and started to say something as she pointed at me with her hand, but the doctor interrupted her with, "The visit costs five rubles."

My mother, in a pleading tone, replied, "No, *Herr Doktor.* I only have three rubles."

• 36 •

She actually had four rubles, but she had put one ruble away for expenses.

Shouting, "I don't soil my hands for three rubles," the doctor flung out of the room, slamming the door.

Grieving and pale, my mother resumed her seat. The tender look she gave me pierced me like hot needles.

The blond woman who had opened the door for us came in. "The doctor doesn't take anyone for less than five rubles. You've wasted your time coming here. I'm sorry."

Reaching into her dress, my mother took a kerchief from between her breasts, unknotted it, and took out a couple of bills and some small change.

With trembling fingers, she counted the money over. There were four rubles, no more.

Putting all the money into the blond woman's hand, she said, "Go on. Give it to the doctor. Let him save my poor boy." She gathered me up in her arms and squeezed me to her breast. Her voice tearful, she said, "You see, it's not good to be poor."

The blond woman went out. A few moments later she was back. Standing in the doorway, she said, "Go on in. *Herr Doktor* will see your boy."

It was a frosty winter day in late February. The town seemed to be bound with white chains.

When we left the doctor's house, the cold was more intense than it had been before. A powdery snow flew about every which way in stinging gusts, as if the breath of the frozen earth would not permit the snow to fall on it and was continually chasing it back up to the heights.

Silently my mother held my hand. We walked on for a long while, still silently.

I grew tired of looking at the houses, the shop windows, the droshkies, the cars, and the sleighs.

I wanted terribly to eat something.

"Momma, I'm hungry."

She heaved a sigh but said nothing.

For an hour or two we wandered about in the cold. I felt my mother's hand turning to ice. Her face was extremely pale, like the freezing snow.

"Why aren't we going home?" I asked. "We've already been to the doctor."

Then suddenly I understood. My mother had given all of her money to the doctor. After that I no longer said I was hungry, but kept still like my mother.

In this silent fashion we moved about the town, down one street, up another.

Why didn't my mother let go of my hand, since she seemed to be almost frozen?

"Momma, Momma. You're cold."

She didn't answer. Tears welled up in her eyes, and she moved straight ahead silently, like the blind who feel their way with their fingers. It seemed to me that her lips moved as if she were praying.

I felt like crying, but I knew that my tears would only add to my mother's pain. So I restrained myself and was still like my mother.

The bright reflected light hurt my eyes. My head was buzzing. The cold made me hungry. I sensed that my mother avoided looking at me. But her freezing hand pressed ever harder on mine. That cold pressure told me how great was her grief and how much she loved me.

We were beginning to walk more and more slowly. When my mother's lips moved now, I could clearly hear her prayers.

In her old-fashioned, long black coat, dotted with its faded mother-of-pearl buttons; with her frayed shawl from whose folds her snow white face looked out; and with her wide, prayerful eyes and her delicate, delicate measured pace, she might have been taken for some otherworldly creature.

She came to a stop at a busy intersection and, for a moment or two, watched the people who passed by. Then she put out her small white hand into the cold air. Slowly, silently, deliberately, she put her hand out to the passersby.

The town seemed to me to turn hostile and strange. The

thousands of gleaming specks made by the gas and electric lights in the streets, in the windows, on the droshkies and cars glowered at me now with the blazing eyes of demons.

A few groschen fell into my mother's hand, and each groschen seemed to freeze a tear in her large unhappy eyes. I buried myself in the soft folds of her dress. Feeling miserable and abandoned on that frozen street, I pressed myself against her, hiding my face as I wept, without words, without sounds.

It seemed to me that every groschen the generous passersby dropped into my mother's hand gave a dull, choked echo, as if it had struck some frozen thing.

"Momma, Momma, are you cold?" I asked.

There was no answer. She did not look at me. Rigid, freezing, she stood with her hand outstretched and begged.

And now I felt the way I had then. Felt the same strangeness, the same loneliness. I had the same sense that I was being regarded by everyone with hostility, with the sort of look that walls give you when you have walked inadvertently into a house in which you once lived. Or the scornful, baleful look you get from mirrors when you happen to meet their glance as you pass by.

Suddenly I was aware that the last bit of humanity I still possessed was dying in me. And I trembled at the thought that I might be seen standing at street corners, repeating hoarsely various lies—that I had been paralyzed or severely wounded in the war. After which I would beg for food or a handout of a couple of groschen.

In recent days I had harassed and tormented myself, threatening: *You'll see. You'll turn into a beggar, into a thief.* And so on. Such thoughts made me blush for shame. My whole body seemed to burn. Had anyone else accused me of half the iniquities of which I accused myself, I would have leaped at him, fists swinging.

It's strange, how one can believe oneself to be an absolute nothing, can attack and insult oneself and at the same time be consumed by self-love.

I detested liars. I had been too lonely and had suffered too much to want to add being a liar to the list. I despised liars—those people who made things up out of whole cloth, who bragged, who elevated themselves to the skies.

And yet I did tell lies—to myself and to others. I imagined untrue things. It might happen like this: walking along the street, in the heat and dust, scorched by the sun, there could occur to me, out of the blue and provoked by God alone knows what, some wild, queer tale involving myself. The tale was always fantastic, always bizarre.

I used to wonder where the stories came from which, on bright sunny days, on a street alive with people, popped into my head. Such frightful, savage tales, and in such horrifying colors. Then I would smile like someone suddenly remembering what was clear to him long ago: *Ah ha! The tale comes to you from one of your dreams, but you don't remember*. And for a little while I was willing to think it had come from a dream, from a recent dream. But later I would have to admit that I was lying. I had never dreamed any such thing. Then, tenaciously, over several hours, I would try to prove that I *had* dreamed it. Even as I argued with myself, I knew I was lying. Strange how powerful is the need to demonstrate that a lie is the pure truth.

Those wild tales, made up out of whole cloth, filled me with such fierce energy that I forgot everything else.

Often several such tales would enter my mind at the same time. But not in any order. Where one ended, the other did not necessarily begin. No. Sometimes one tale included the other. The second could intrude into the third, the third into the first, and so on. As in *The Tale of a Thousand and One Nights*.

The stories that came to me were tales of love, of hate, of disgust. Sometimes, walking in the streets, I would grow dizzy with revulsion. Some of the wilder tales were so very funny that I could find myself walking in a trance and laughing all the while.

Let me tell you one such tale.

9

One day, passing down a narrow street, a very narrow street, I felt terribly hungry. I had no money. As I reached the middle of the block I noticed a bakery. In the doorway, which was itself wider than the street, there stood an impossibly fat woman. Amused, I studied her from a distance, thinking first that she was no doubt the owner of the bakery and second that, if I chose to steal a few loaves of bread from her, she was so fat she would not be able to chase me because she was broader than the street. If she tried running after me, she would topple a couple of houses in her path.

I waste no time in thinking but walk into the shop and ask for seven loaves of bread. She sets seven loaves out for me, but before handing them over she gives me a sharp look. As soon as I get the loaves, I start to make my escape, but no such luck. My shoes turn out to be welded to the floor. Before I can look around, the fat woman grabs me up, tosses me into her apron, and carries me into the other room where there's an oven larger than any I have ever seen, and several baker's apprentices with pointy noses and tiny eyes under their low brows. The fat woman drops me into an empty tub and, repeating a spell, says:

> *Don't you move.*
> *Don't you move.*
> *Don't you move.*

I lie still like one dead. It is instantly clear that the woman is a witch.

"Husband," she says. "Snubnose here [that's my name] just tried to rob us."

"Well, wife, fix him the way we do," replies the oldest of the bakers.

"You do it. Today it's your turn to show what you can do."

Yielding to her, he says, "As you like, wife."

I lie spread-eagled in the tub and look about. The bakers are working with lumps of dough, shaping them to resemble a variety of human shapes. One piece looks like a German soldier, another like a French soldier, still others make Bulgarian, Chinese, or Turkish soldiers, and so on.

Strange, I think. *A new form of pastry.*

Then I notice something new. The five bakers resemble angels. Meanwhile, the work is just whizzing along. Yeast is added, dough is kneaded, implements are scrubbed. Things are shoved into and pulled out of the oven. Then one of the bakers draws a paddleful of baked goods out, and suddenly it occurs to me that I'm in an art bakery. What's on the paddle is very beautiful.

The French soldier, the Englishman with the sideburns, the American with his pipe have come out wonderfully; only the German soldier, the Turk, and the Austrian have been singed by the flames. Actually, their feet have been burned to a crisp. The baker, seeing them, says, "Well, they're not worth a damn."

Then, pointing at me, he says, "Let's do something miraculous with this one." With one hand he snatches me out of the tub; with the other he scoops up some dough, rolls me up in it, and makes a neat loaf over which he sprinkles golden seeds. Then he puts me into the oven, where I am instantly enveloped by flames that both singe and bake me. When I am done, the baker takes me out, dusts me free of ashes, prods me, looks me over, then, taking me over to the window, he says with a smile, "Fly away."

The little golden loaf flies off over fields and rivers, over seas; it flies and flies, night and day, in sunshine and in moonlight, never resting at all. Finally it reaches a country where everyone wears red fezes on their heads; their faces and muscular hands look wrinkled, worn with labor and with grief.

The people in the red fezes, seeing the golden loaf flying over their heads, are overjoyed and send up balloons, hoping to catch it.

But I just keep right on flying, flying, higher and higher into the clouds, toying all the while with the crowd of my pursuers until finally I am caught. And then it is an occasion for the whole country to rejoice.

The loaf was cut into many pieces and divided up among all the people, each of whom ate the bloody morsels of the golden loaf.

That's the sort of queer tale that, in their hundreds, sneaked into the anxious depths of my mind. In broad daylight I was able to dream whole newspapers or radio reports and to envision gigantic billboards in their entirety.

But each of my fantasies made a certain kind of sense, which served to reassure me that I was not yet insane despite the fact that only moments ago bizarre visions had attacked my weary mind. Then my hands had trembled and everything around me had seemed to be receding, turning strange. I can remember very well that after one of those foolish tales had filled me with feverish dread, my eyesight grew weak, things around me blurred, and I felt exactly as if I had just gotten up from a seizure of unconsciousness.

At that time I was sitting in a park, and I kept smelling the fresh odor of oranges. The smell was so strong that I got up to look into the nearby garden to see whether there was an orange tree growing there. Later I remembered that in my strange tale there had been a marvelous orange orchard. Or if I dreamed of a shady countryside, then on the street on which I happened to be walking the sun disappeared and suddenly it was pitch-dark night.

10

Again I did not have a groschen in my pocket. I had used my last few marks to buy some bread and herring which I ate in an entryway. I was full. The heavily salted herring made me very thirsty. My mouth burned, and my parched lips began to crack. I hurried to the park, meaning to get to the well where I could drink my fill of cold water. The clock in the bell tower tolled three times over the town. The sky was a clear blue, and the sun took on the appearance of a midday summer sun.

In the municipal park there were a lot of people sitting on the benches, looking on contentedly as the last rays of the warm sun sprawled on the pebble-strewn yellow earth. I drank deeply at the well. Then, as usual, I sat down on one of the benches and turned my face upward. I grew warm. My toughened skin trembled under the touch of the sun.

There's something sad, something wistful about looking at a place where withered yellow leaves are enfolded in gleaming sunlight. I'll never understand the Christians who dress their dead in the finest clothing. There's something helpless, even foolish, about the dead, but a corpse whose relatives have decked it out in white silk gloves seems especially helpless and foolish.

Across from me sat a young woman. She was engrossed in reading a book. Her head was slightly bent, so that between the book and the top of her head one could see less than half her face. She had a thin, tightly closed mouth and a slender nose with quivering nostrils that were as pale as her small pale cheeks. Clearly she was deeply caught up in her reading. And now I was able to observe that a truly involved reader makes use of more than his or her eyes. Every nerve, every muscle, every fold in her face was reading. The delicate veins in her lovely pale hands pulsed. It was easy enough to imagine that the words she snatched up with her eyes leaped directly into her bloodstream, where they danced about in her veins.

Just then she reached into her purse for a handkerchief with which she touched her eyes. Yes, she was crying. Then she raised her head. Two huge, dark, tear-filled eyes looked at me. Embarrassed, she got quickly to her feet and hurried away. She was chagrined because I had noticed her tears.

How long had it been since I had held a book in my hands? I could hardly remember. I felt terribly hungry for a book—famished, the way one might be for food. I felt that I would read anything at all in the way of a book without regard to its contents. I would read anything, swallowing every letter on whatever bit of printed paper.

Then I felt myself being observed by a pair of sharp eyes. I turned. There, standing above me, was a tall, clean-shaven man whose eyes had the half-closed look that one sees in people who are in the theater.

Seeing that I had noticed him, he signaled to me and said, "Pssst."

I got to my feet and went quickly over to him.

"Do you want to earn some money?" he asked. "If so, then come with me." He turned and, without waiting for me to reply, started off toward the street.

I went after him, cheered by the prospect of earning some money. It made no difference to me what I might be asked to do. Anything. I was willing to do anything at all.

We went on for several blocks. In all that time the man turned only once to look at me. The streets here were becoming livelier. Clusters of workers went by, all of them engaged in angry conversations. I had no idea what was causing the excitement.

Passing the building in which were the editorial offices of a newspaper, things became clearer. In the large window hung a huge sign on which, printed in block letters, was the message: TEXTILE GENERAL STRIKE. When the man I was with glimpsed the sign, he smiled and said, "That will be cheerful. The weavers' strike."

When we had gone some distance away from the park, he led me into the huge building that housed the circus. In the foyer, he opened a door without bothering to knock.

We went into a small room all of whose walls were stuck over with placards. On every wall there were pictures of "champions" showing off their massive muscular chests: of iron twisters, of elephants, tigers, lions, and other wild animals. All the beasts had their mouths wide open, ready to devour.

There was no furniture in the room except for an ancient threadbare sofa on which lay outstretched a thickset man with a brick red face.

"I've got you one, *Herr Direktor*," said the man I had been following.

"Good."

"Tell him what he'll make."

"Two thousand. Four hours. And both of you, get yourselves out of here." The manager jumped to his feet and pushed us from the room.

"You'll get two thousand marks for going about the streets carrying this little gimmick," he said, pointing to a thin board nailed to a long stick to which was pasted a sign on which was displayed the huge head of a tiger in a ferocious pose, its mouth wide open, displaying a set of sharp white teeth. In its eyes was a bloodthirsty, ravenous glitter. Beneath the tiger, in black letters, was written: CIRCUS VANGOLI. TWELVE BENGAL TIGERS. FINAL WEEK. HALF PRICE.

Without a word I took up the placard with the tiger on it. It was not much of a burden.

"Go about in the main streets where there are crowds of people."

I started off. I was a stranger in the town, and, except for a couple of chance acquaintances, I knew nobody, so I had no worries that I would be seen doing this not entirely respectable work.

In any case, I couldn't care less whether I was seen or not. I carried the "savage" tiger with both hands and walked straight on, constantly in danger of being run over by crowds of automobiles, trucks, and droshkies. I had a feeling of well-being and walked with a certain solemnity as I reminded myself that I was now earning money. I started to think of what I would buy once I had been paid my first wages. What I would do, first of all, would be to go to the flea market, where I would buy myself a colored shirt and an old book. One could buy such things there for a few groschen.

As I walked, I remembered the pale young woman I had seen in the park, the one whose eyes filled with tears as she read her book. More than anything else I recalled her pale, weeping hands. Yes, weeping hands! And I felt again the yearning to read a book. I began to imagine the ordinary letters of the alphabet as enclosed in light and as having human characteristics. The letter *aleph* resembled an angry stepfather who sits in his daddy chair and never moves from his place; *gimel*, like a badly looked after tubercular; *zayin*, like a boy wearing a cap with visors on both sides; and *lamed*, like a good lamb with a neck that is too thin and long.

How I loved those letters! As I walked, I read with strange delight every printed word that came my way: WOMEN'S TAILOR—SILBERFA- DEN. PARFUMERIE SCHATSKY. I read and I read, indefatigably swallowing words with my eyes, endlessly, ravenously, unable to get my fill.

It was now quite warm. Before the painted doors of restaurants slick-haired waiters wearing white shirts and polished shoes stood taking a breathing spell, as if they were airing away the smells of meat, mustard, herring, and fish that had penetrated not only their clothes but into their very bones. The smell of smoke wafted down from the chimneys of the tall buildings. Everywhere there was a noisy racket of tramways, automobiles, and droshkies, mingling with the various shouts of newsboys calling the names of their papers and the evening's news. The smell of asphalt was strong in the air, as well as the smell of axle grease, which, in the heat of the day, melted and dripped from the wheels of the trucks and the wagons onto the filthy paving stones of the road.

To the usual flow of pedestrians—merchants, sales agents, and street peddlers—was now added the influx of a crowd of scowling weavers who hurried along the sidewalks, their brows wrinkled as they carried on excited or heated discussions. The store owners along the street stood before their shops, doing what they could to hide their fear as they tried to read the sallow, withered faces of the passing weavers. In some shops the owners were testing whether the metal shutters over their windows were in order, whether, if needed, they would drop easily into place.

At the intersections reinforced police patrols moved about, watching the embittered weavers with a chill sympathy, the way one looks at someone who is just showing symptoms of a mental breakdown: any minute now and it will be necessary to pack him off to a madhouse. The police marched more briskly, turning now here, now there, stamping their boots on the coarsely cemented cobblestones.

One of them approached a group of workers that had paused under a street lamp and were about to start a discussion. "Break it up, folks. Break it up."

The workers moved apart, but slowly, lazily. I moved along stiffly, ceremoniously, carrying my Bengal tiger like a lamp carrier at a Christian funeral. Together with horses, wagons, tramways, I strode along in the middle of the street, my tiger blazing.

The number of workers increased at every moment, and their discussions were now more intense, more heated—more painful. The crowds of boneless, puffy-faced merchants, agents, and stockbrokers had evaporated like water from the sidewalks, and their places had been taken by weavers in grease-stained work clothes and shoes with heavy wooden soles into which steel taps or heavy nails had been driven. On all sides the sounds of steel striking cobblestones could be heard. The sallow-faced, bright-eyed, embittered weavers repeated at intervals, "Director Zavadsky. Bloodsucker. Scoundrel. Director Zavadsky."

The name Zavadsky flew from mouth to mouth, from one man to another, from one woman to another, always with bitter anger, spoken through clenched teeth or in mockery. Men were abusive; women called down curses.

The crowd of men and women were massed on both sidewalks of the long main street. When they first got there, the weavers had felt themselves uneasy in the expensive neighborhood and looked about warily, like newcomers to a strange town. They stared at the shop windows, at the stucco columns before the buildings, at the painted zinc roofs, at the polished windowpanes that were enveloped by woven garlands of leaves, laurel branches, and large fall flowers. At first the weavers tried to keep down the noise made by their wooden soles, but as their numbers increased, their mood became more relaxed, more familiar, and they set their feet down more energetically on the stones of the unfamiliar street. The massed, serpentine column of workers extended as far as the eye could see. And now they felt themselves secure, at home—so much so that they began to make jokes about the bosses, about the inhabitants of the street.

A black automobile in which sat two elegantly clad, thickset men, glided down the street.

"A couple of Zavadsky's wallet partners." The venomous remark came from someone in the crowd.

"Sons of bitches," said a tall, blond young weaver.

The car disappeared.

My tiger was sometimes noticed and sometimes ignored. People's minds were on something else. On the other hand, I was not myself much concerned with the striking weavers. I was waiting for the hours to pass so that I could return my tiger to the circus.

Suddenly I was shaken by an asthmatic cry that sounded in the midst of the street. A ragged old woman weaver with dark, bony, troll-like features had set herself on the tracks some ten paces before an oncoming trolley car.

"Stop! The bourgeoisie doesn't move another inch. Go tell the world, go tell them all that the weavers are perishing with hunger."

The tram driver managed to stop the tramway just in time to avoid a disaster. From the sidewalks there was a surge of workers, who in their thousands gathered around and enveloped the tram.

The frightened passengers alighted from the cars as if there *had* been an accident.

"Dear lady," the motorman said, trying to calm the old woman. "The bourgeoisie doesn't ride on streetcars. The rich travel in automobiles."

Holding on to my placard with both hands, I found myself crushed by the thousands of workers, who with a single will were pressing in on the blocked tram.

After considerable exhortation, the clever motorman succeeded in persuading the old woman to get off the tracks.

Slowly, carefully, he maneuvered his car through the packed crowd.

"Ah, the poor weavers. It's not enough that the war has killed your sons. Now Zavadsky's trying to take the bit of bread from your mouths."

"There are thirty thousand of us hanging about without work. And now he wants to drive the rest of us out of the factories. He wants to reduce us to beggary."

"We're not going to take it in silence. We won't let him!"

"Down with the sons of whores!"

"Death to Director Zavadsky!"

On the sidewalks and in the street, the waves of a sea of angry faces swelled and surged. There was not so much as a hairsbreadth of space among the massed bodies. Heads everywhere. Heads, and eyes blazing with furious hatred. Heads framed in blond . . . in dark hair. Grizzled heads and the heads of women young and old. And every head in motion. Excited. Angry. Snatches of words escaped from between compressed lips or clenched teeth. Incendiary phrases flew through the air, collided with each other, mingled, then faded in confusion, only to be repeated once more in the same turbulent shout rising from the same commotion. And proudly looking down on the entire scene—the heads in feverish motion, the expensive facades of the houses, the balconies and terraces—was my Bengal tiger with his people-hating maw wide open, and the message, written in plump black letters that glistened in the sunlight: CIRCUS VANGOLI. TWELVE BENGAL TIGERS. FINAL WEEK. HALF PRICE.

The iron shutters over the shop windows were hastily lowered; rusted wrought-iron grillwork was slammed shut. The shouts of the weavers were lost in the general racket. Then suddenly, without a gesture or a signal from anyone, the massed heads stirred into a single motion, and I felt myself hemmed in by ribs, breasts, hands, and shoulders. Unable to move, I was immersed in a human sea.

From all sides came the cry, "To his house! To Director Zavadsky's!"

And I was caught up and dragged along in the flow of the colossal crowd on its way to Director Zavadsky's house.

Frightened faces, half hidden behind shades or curtains, were beginning to appear in the windows of the wealthier homes on the way. They peered out on every side and, seeing my sign, shrugged their shoulders, perplexed, not understanding how a circus had anything to do with what was going on. We moved through a number of streets, actually passing the theater building on our way. There I caught a glimpse of the circus manager, who was standing at one of the windows beside the man who had spoken to me in the park.

Seeing the placard and the vastness of the crowd, the manager laughed with such pleasure that his whole body shook.

Two streets later the movement of the crowd came to a stop. Kneeling down, I could see that the first ranks of the marchers, who were a considerable distance from me, were pressing in on a four-story house that had before it a wrought-iron fence enclosing a garden shaded by a couple of slender acacia trees.

"Director Zavadsky! Let him come out! We want Director Zavadsky!"

It's interesting how much pleasure workers take in seeing the man they regard as their enemy. All cats, even those on a leash, dance with excitement when they see a mouse—no matter how far away.

The iron gate was closed.

"Zavadsky! Zavadsky! Director Zavadsky!" The intensity of the shouting increased.

For a moment or two longer the crowd shouted and yelled, "Zavadsky. Zavadsky."

On a second-floor balcony a door opened. A man in his fifties, with lined, stern features, appeared, trembling with fear.

The crowd grew still, every eye fixed on the man on the balcony. For a couple of seconds he looked down at the sea of faces. "Workers! Are you here because you want to know whether you can come back to work?"

"No!" came the threatening interruption from the crowd.

"Have you come to hear me tell you the facts: that the Polish textile industry, because of the tricks of our enemies, has practically lost all of its export market; and that the war has so impoverished our own citizens that they cannot buy the output of our factories?"

From the frightened sound of his voice it was clear that he would have preferred to talk in quite another fashion.

It is a fact frequently observed that in unsettling or frightening circumstances, one can sometimes sustain an artificial calm by self-imitation. To put the matter more clearly, a person at such moments becomes an actor repeating word by word the same things—the same phrases, including even the same pauses, that served him once at some special moment in his life.

This was now the case with Zavadsky, who would much rather have said something more appropriate. But, overmastered by fear, all he could bring himself to do was to repeat familiar lines and phrases. And so he plunged on: "And to reduce the labor force . . . "

The phrase ended the crowd's attentiveness. At first there were a number of outcries mingled with each other, then there were others, increasing in volume, until finally the angry bellowing of a gigantic ox was heard.

"You've put twenty thousand workers out on the streets!"

"Murderer of workers' children!"

"Son of a whore!"

Zavadsky turned pale and pretended not to hear. Summoning all his strength, he tried to resume his speech—and succeeded. The mob grew silent once more.

"Workers! The Polish textile industry, which was shattered by the German occupation, has made a considerable recovery, thanks to the tenacity and the endurance of the manufacturers and workers."

"Right! You built new factories with *our* money," cried a voice in the crowd.

"For the various reasons I have already indicated, a number of workers . . . " And here he hesitated, but it was his bad luck to *find* the word for which he appeared to be searching—the word he meant to attach to the last link in the chain of words he had already spoken. ". . . a number of workers . . . are superfluous."

The mob shuddered with contempt, with rage. Yells, shouts rose to the skies. Thousands of arms stretched out; thousands of hands, balled into fists, were shaken in anger and indignation as a furious answering cry went up: "Superfluous! Who's superfluous? You dogs. You're the ones who are superfluous in the world. Loafers. Scoundrels. Bloodsuckers. Superfluous!"

The crowd's blind anger toward Zavadsky made it impossible for it to grasp or to tolerate the innocent sense of what he had said. Their hostility seethed and intensified, as if the sea of people had been caught up in an electrical storm. Curses and shouts tore incoherently into the air, as if from drunken throats.

Suddenly someone tore up a paving stone from the street and flung it high into the air. There was the sound of shattering glass. People on the sidewalk edged away from where the broken glass had fallen. Director Zavadsky, his face pale as death, turned and ran from the balcony.

Just as the smell of blood gets carnivores wildly excited, just so does the sound of breaking glass excite a revolutionary crowd. Stones now flew like hail in a storm. Splinters of glass covered the sidewalk before Zavadsky's house, and shattered glass was everywhere on the asphalt. The people who had been there minutes before suddenly disappeared. The twenty-thousand-headed mob responded to the sound of breaking glass with wild yells and bizarre curses. The people were compacted now into a mass resembling a raging, roaring beast. A dozen times groups of workers tried to tear down the iron gates, but, cursing, wiping sweat from their faces, they had to retreat from the impossible task.

All at once, as if erupting from the ground, thousands of white leaflets flew into the air. Thousands of proclamations were passed quickly into thousands of outstretched hands. I glanced at one in someone's hand: "The Polish Communist Workers Party" was printed at the bottom of the leaflets. The name was underlined in black.

When there was not a single unbroken window in the second story, the crowd calmed down a bit. All at once someone began to sing. And now twenty thousand voices, hoarse from shouting and cursing, took up the song. As if the song was a signal, the mass of workers started moving again, forming a great linked chain jingling along as they shouted and sang their way through the main avenues.

Then, without warning, one of the workers grabbed the handle of my placard and with a piece of blue chalk scrawled "Director Zavadsky" above my tiger's head and crossed out "Circus Vangoli." Until that moment my placard had been little noticed. But now it became the target of everyone's delighted and raucous attention.

And that's how the Bengal tiger became "Director Zavadsky."

The sky darkened. The gentle rumblings of autumn thunder could be heard, followed by a hasty, scattered rain. The blue chalk on my placard was washed away, and my tiger became once again the true Bengal tiger of the Circus Vangoli. For another few moments the crowd followed my placard. Then it began to fragment, dispersing into all parts of the town.

11

A blue evening sifted down from the sky through a fine slanting rain. The chill drops exhaled a pale mist that enclosed the town in a dim veil that refracted the light from thousands of lamps in houses and from auto, tram, and droshky headlights, making them seem distant—very distant—to the eye.

It's strange how anyone who has to do considerable walking on the streets of a town gets to be familiar with horses. Their enormous eyes look into one's own with such intimacy, with such comradely feeling that they seem to be saying something, uttering some kind of mute greeting. Because I was constantly on the alert to avoid being run down, I developed the keen sense of smell of a police dog. It was my nose that first told me that horses were stumbling behind me. I could tell the difference between the smells of an auto and those of a tram. It happened frequently that, as I carried the placard of the Bengal tiger in both hands, I would catch a compassionate glimpse in the eye of a passing horse. Sympathy for me, a human.

There were a number of lighted lamps hanging high up on the wall of the Circus Vangoli, all of them in a variety of shrieking colors that were meant to entice the public.

I went in. The manager, seeing me, smiled in a friendly way. When he smiled, his eyes, except for the bright gleam that showed through the slits, were swallowed by the folds of his eyelids.

"I really like this guy," he said, indicating me to a small man who stood beside him. "Twenty thousand weavers advertised my circus. The town may have thought the weavers were striking in my favor. That's what you call a real double Nelson. My word! Ha, ha, ha! It was hilarious watching the tiger keeping pace with the weavers. You had to hold your sides to keep from cracking up." The two men laughed. "Young fellow," the manager said, slapping me on the shoulder in a friendly way, "you deserve a bonus. A medal. Stick with me and you'll go far. Higher and higher. You see that guy over there?" He pointed at a man with blond hair who was just leaving the cashier's office. "He used to be a nobody. A good-for-nothing, hungry for a bite to eat. He used to go slinking off after acrobats so he could shine their shoes. But I took a liking to him, and since then he's come up in the world. Up and up. You know what he is now? He's my business manager. Do you know what that means? Business manager of the Circus Vangoli, to which the town president, the millionaire Poznansky, himself comes several times a month? And Oskar Kon, both of whom admire my apes—I mean my tigers. Take it from me, young fellow, you'll go up in the world. Because of you, twenty thousand men advertised my business. Now you take that tiger and put him somewhere backstage."

I asked a worker how to get backstage, and he showed me the way. I found a place for the placard and then returned to the lobby.

Two or three hours before a performance, a theater lobby has an early morning, sleepy look to it. The sort of sleepiness that seems to be poured over a room in which people are getting up to go to work, stumbling about looking for their clothes or splashing water on their faces.

In the circus the great lamps burn with a haughty, if empty and foolish, light staring down at their own theater folk who are moving about in all directions. Since the lamps are unneeded, their intense light is squandered freely on the brightly painted walls. In the checkroom, the naked coatracks and shelves stare—waiting. The outside dark peeps in through the circus's open doors and steals for itself a few of the beams from the lamps blazing in the lobby. And in the interior, a thick shaft of dust receives enough light so that it is transformed into a bright obelisk that cuts through the auditorium.

The smells, the exhalations of thousands and thousands of people who, over weeks, over years, have sat for hours at a stretch in these seats, seep out, recalling rot and death.

The ticket booth is open, and if not enough money comes in, the manager gets gloomy and irritable.

There is no one in the world who imitates a boss quite as slavishly as a theater employee imitates his manager. The most minor employee of a theater, circus, or movie house who has worked, say, for a full ten years, will have, both in his character and in his features, certain aspects of his manager. In every theater there's sure to be one employee who looks just like the manager's brother. And should it happen that the box office fails to take in enough money, so that the manager is grumpy, why then the cashier and the ticket taker and the porter, everyone from the lowest to the highest is grumpy too. With a single glance at the number of seats occupied in the house, the most minor employee can tell with the precision of the cashier exactly how much money has come in.

Money talks. It may be a low sort of speech, a jargon, but it speaks loudly. Doli, the little humpbacked clown with whom I later became acquainted, was able to deduce simply from a man's gestures, his mien, and his tone of voice exactly how much the fellow earned per week and the amount of his pension. After giving him a single sly glance, he unhesitatingly said, "You're not earning more than eighty or ninety a week, and when you buy fourth-row tickets, it puts a heavy strain on your pocketbook. You'd do better to sit in the gallery."

Later, Doli confided, "The fellow's in love with one of our woman acrobats, so he tries to give the impression that he's a rich man."

I wandered about, peering into every room and corner, examining scaffolds and all sorts of other circus gear.

Following a long corridor on whose filthy, sweating walls hung two red lamps, I strayed into the menagerie. There were twelve tigers lying about in iron cages, four tigers to a cage. Several of the beasts slept, snoring like aging asthmatics, or as if felled by heavy labor. Two of them rested their heads on their forepaws and regarded me while they pretended to be dead. Slime from their nostrils oozed onto their whiskers. My sudden appearance in the dark made not the slightest impression on them. Ten of them, lying on their backs, snored, and the other two watched me through nearly closed eyes, as if I were an old acquaintance. The nauseating smell of feces, wafted to me from these African princesses, was like the smell that comes from the rubber-sheeted beds of old people waiting to die.

All the tigers were more or less dark yellow in color, with spots on their throats. The greenish glow in the eyes of the two half-slumbering beasts that were watching me cut through the dark. For the most part, they looked like huge toothless old cats who were no longer able to kill mice.

I was curious to see what sorts of tricks Jackson, the famous tiger tamer, could make these twelve lazy, sleepy, exhausted Bengal tigers perform.

Looking at these wild beasts depressed me. Feeling ill at ease, I left the menagerie.

At the buffet, a thickly powdered older woman was sorting piles of candy and sandwiches. As she turned to a young woman standing near her, she counted with the tip of her forefinger: "Six, seven . . . eighteen, nineteen . . ."

The young woman wrote it down.

The silence spread over everything. It rocked itself in the plush overstuffed chairs. The bored windows glimmered dreamily.

The sandwiches reminded me that I was hungry. Suddenly I was ravenous again. But my various duties in the circus kept me busy, and I was unable to get out into the street.

It was night. I saw no way to find a little money, so I went back to the twelve tigers. At my second arrival one of the tigers opened an eye, looked me over, yawned a wide yawn, then rested its head once more on its paws. The others kept right on sleeping. From the menagerie I returned once more backstage, and from there to the lobby. I wandered about for a while, now in one place, now in another.

Backstage there was a stagehand sitting on the step of a ladder eating his supper. When he was done eating, I went up to him and asked how much bread cost.

He was a simple Pole, with a long mustache. He replied, "Seven hundred marks." Just to make conversation, I said that if one used ovens imported from America, ovens that used electricity, the cost of making bread would come down. He smoothed his mustache and expressed amazement. Then I asked the prices of other things. How much was a pound of coffee? Of tea? He knew what they cost by heart. "Coffee, thirty-five thousand per pound. Tea, seventeen thousand a quarter of a pound. Cooking barley, seven hundred."

Listening to the prices made me feel like someone from a foreign land. As I left him, I asked myself, *What do these numbers mean to you?* Hunger was gnawing at me.

"Why is it," I accused myself, "that you haven't got any acquaintances from whom you could borrow a little money?"

I went backstage once more and looked for the stagehand. On the pretense that we had once met elsewhere, I asked him to remind me of his name.

"Joseph Fornall," he said. Then, looking at me, he shook his head and said, "No. I don't know you."

"Where do you live?"

He told me.

"You're sure you don't know me?"

"No. I've never seen you before in my life." He stared.

"You don't remember?"

"No, I can't remember at all."

I asked a further question or two, hoping to provoke something that would prove he knew me. Then I left, dismayed.

In the lobby, I ran into the manager. He had a pipe in his mouth from which he puffed whole clouds of smoke. He started to go backstage. I went up to him and asked for some money.

"You've got it! I owe it to you. Yes," he said, puffing again on his pipe. His words, jostling their way past the mouthpiece, were thick, unclear. He gave me two ten-thousand-mark bills. They dazzled me. I grabbed the money and went out into the street, then into a store where I bought bread, sausage, and cigarettes. Then, when I was full, I went for a walk. A fine rain was falling, but it did not bother anyone. Men and women dressed in holiday clothing were strolling on both sides of the street.

Cheered by my full belly, I walked more quickly. But my recent headache did not stop. Evidently it was indifferent to the great hunk of bread and the sausage I had eaten.

I had a lighted cigarette in my mouth as I strolled with my hands in my pockets. There were a couple of women walking ahead of me. One of them, a slightly stocky woman with broad shoulders, had very beautiful feet. As she walked, she took small, energetic steps. She frequently turned her head nervously from side to side, so that, though I walked behind her, I could see her broad, heavily powdered face and the fleshy mound of her downy double chin. She had a wholesome, instinctive smile that seemed to stretch from ear to ear.

I felt the blood rush to my face. My heart began to beat more quickly.

The second woman was shorter and thinner. I followed them both, absolutely drunk with passion. One of the women, the smaller one, noticed me following them. She looked scared and whispered something to her friend who looked back at me. She too took fright. She grabbed her friend's arm and they both started off, walking fast.

Though the fear in their faces had a dampening effect, I could not tear myself away, and went after them. Several times they looked back. Finally one of them yanked her friend by the arm and they took refuge by going—no, running—into a café. I was left standing in the street like a fool. Furious, I punched a wall with my fist, then hurried away.

For ten minutes or so I wandered about in the streets. Then I went back to the circus. I did not forget to buy a newspaper, which with trembling hand I put in my inside coat pocket. I didn't want to read the paper in the street. Back at the circus, I would find myself some cozy spot—the sort of place one can find backstage. There I would read the newspaper from beginning to end.

When I returned to the circus, the performance had already begun. I went in through the stage entrance. The porter knew me by now as an employee. I went up to the first balcony and watched the show. There were perhaps a thousand people in the auditorium. Rich, well-dressed men and women sat in the lower loges and waited impatiently for the acts to proceed. There was a feverish anticipation in the eyes of the heavily powdered women. The rest of the audience consisted for the most part of workers, their weary eyes bright with hunger and a desire to be entertained. From the galleries could be heard hoarse voices and the continual sound of nuts cracking. Below there was a rustling of silks and satins and the snapping of chocolate bars.

All at once ten new spotlights went on and five reflectors created a fantastic bright blue light in the auditorium, light in whose glow the pale powdered faces framed in shawls or in silk or satin hats looked like wax dolls.

There was a vigorous drumroll and Doli, the dwarf, the "Lilliputian Clown," appeared. He was slowly hoisted ten meters into the air at the tip of a pole, which made it seem that he was rising out of the ground. Doli looked at the audience, made a face like a frog's, and started to cry. As he wept, he really looked like a monster with the face of a frog. His face was green, and tears, in two streams, rolled like peas down his cheeks and fell to the sand-strewn ground. The women grimaced and looked on with fascinated revulsion, watching him through mother-of-pearl and silver lorgnettes.

In the gallery people hooted and shouted:

"Hey, you devil."

"Monster!"

"Doli, you sorcerer."

"Monkey."

Doli wept for ten minutes or so—sometimes like a hungry child, sometimes like an old man. Sometimes he wept like a woman, sometimes like a man. His grief rose to a crescendo—and always the two streams of tears flowed down his face.

Then he began to laugh. Swiftly, wildly, hysterically, until, as before, his tears flowed. He laughed through his tears; he mourned hilariously. Sometimes his laughter was delicate, tinkling, tender as a child's or a young girl's. Sometimes it was gross, uncouth, like the laughter from the sick lungs of an alcoholic.

Then his tears stopped and laughter seized the audience. At first it was the people in the gallery that laughed; after that those in the balcony; and finally the genteel well-dressed folk sitting in the loges and in the front rows.

"Doli, you sorcerer."

"Monster."

"Monkey."

"Plague take you."

The auditorium rocked with laughter. Everyone—those on the benches, those in chairs—everyone laughed. A rain of oranges and candies descended on Doli. One woman flung her silk handkerchief at the dwarf.

Doli, however, stared fixedly at a single point somewhere high above his head and entirely ignored the things that fell around him. His mouth wide, he continued to laugh. Then suddenly he stuck out his long tongue and vanished—as if into a grave.

There was a storm of applause in the circus auditorium. From the gallery, renewed terms of endearment for Doli: "Doli, you devil. Monster. Monkey!"

The orchestra began to play. The light reflectors were turned off. The applause subsided. And yet the sound of the clown's laughter seemed still to be hovering in the air.

In one of the rings of the circus there now appeared a man in a frock coat. The music stopped. The man bowed politely and said, "French wrestling matches. International tournament. World champions of Europe, Asia, and Africa. First prize, ten thousand Swiss francs." He bowed again and quickly left the ring.

The light reflectors were turned on again and sixteen gigantic half-naked wrestlers with mountainous chests and muscular arms and legs came out. One of them was black. The wrestlers paraded about the hall in time to the music, displaying their bodies as they marched. A strong odor, as of horses, spread throughout the auditorium—the smell of a muscular stallion. The pale woman wearing the small silk hat (like that of a Franciscan priest) who had thrown her handkerchief at Doli the clown twitched her nostrils and her breasts rose. The naked bodies of the sixteen enormous "world champions of Europe, Asia, and Africa" were encased in the armor of the audience's collective gaze.

The "referee"—the ringmaster—a small compact Jew who wore a frock coat, introduced each of the giants to the audience.

"Gerhard Karsh, German Hercules, champion from the Hartz Mountains. Weight: two hundred forty kilos. Height: one meter ninety three." Compared to the giant, the ringmaster looked as puny as a fly. The German Hercules, hearing his name called, stepped out of the lineup of Gargantuas, bowed deeply before the audience, and smiled as he made his biceps twitch.

"Hadji Vainura. Manchurian. Champion of Mongolia. Weight: two hundred thirty kilos. Height: one meter eighty."

Then the black, expanding his chest, stepped forward, setting his massive, copper-colored feet down forcefully, as if he meant to tear up the floor. For a few moments he looked proudly, unsmilingly— almost with hostility—at the crowd.

"Josef Havlicek, Czechoslovak, weight, one hundred nineteen kilos.

"Gustav af Nestrem, Finland.

"Stepan Pinsky, Poland.

"Ivan Vashminkov, Siberia."

The women in the orchestra seats sniffed the air the way carnivores respond to the smell of blood. The sixteen naked bodies with their massive musculature stirred various lusts in the auditorium. A desire for pain and struggle, for battle, for conquest. In the galleries the exhausted eyes of the striking weavers glittered. In the orchestra seats and in the loges women cuddled up to their male escorts. The pale faces of the merchants and bookkeepers and secretaries crimsoned and were filmed over with the nervous midnight sweat of a lustful sleepless convict.

"Today," the referee announced, "Gerhard Karsh will fight Salvadore Bamboula."

There was a roar, and the German Hercules stepped forward. Then Bamboula, the black man, took his place opposite him. The German threw a punch at Bamboula that caught him on the nape of the neck, producing first a spot and then a flow of blood down the dark skin, and the battle was fully joined.

The German, enormously tall, colossal in his girth, gnawed at his lower lip. He moved his arms about, making kneading motions with his hands as he maneuvered to seize the black by the neck or around the waist.

The stocky black breathed heavily. He panted, and his entire body was drenched with sweat. He stood, immovable as a wall, using his great fists cleverly and skillfully to ward off every attempt the German made to grab him. Karsh threw a body blow at Bambouli.

"Hadjah—hah!" the black man roared in his secret language. Swiftly he grabbed the German from behind and threw him to the ground, then flung his own huge weight across him. The German gasped, choked as if he could not breathe. "My head! My head! Let me up, you black devil!"

"Hey . . . hey," Bamboula muttered exultantly and landed a blow with his fist on the nape of the German's flushed neck.

"Ugh . . .ugh," the German gasped, his arms and legs thrashing the way a hooked fish thrashes with its tail. For a few seconds he lay still, mustering all his strength. Then, erupting like a storm, he did a backward flip and had the black pinned under him.

The German had won. There was violent applause. Smiles everywhere and kisses blown to the victor—who, his hands crossed over his chest, bowed before them all.

12

The performance was over. The audience dispersed. I was alone in the huge circus building. I could hear the doors of the place being locked. It was dark. Very dark. I poked about everywhere in the three-story structure, rummaging for a cozy place where I might lie down. My bones still ached from my last night in the street, and I wanted simply to throw myself down somewhere and fall asleep. I crept into a loge on the first floor, shoved several upholstered chairs together, and stretched out.

Lying there, I thought, *Thank God. Found a place to sleep for the night.* The darkness in the huge space felt oppressive, heavy. I couldn't sleep. My head was full of strange thoughts. Not only that—it was cold. To warm up, I wrapped my coat over my head and started to breathe deeply, quickly. It helped. I was a trifle warmer. I dozed off. Actually, it was a rather heavy doze, but not what one could rightly call sleep. I closed my eyes so as not to have to see the dark, and I prayed for sleep. An hour went by in this fashion. I lay dozing, thinking, but not really sleeping.

In that state, half asleep, half awake, there flashed into my mind a series of images of various experiences I had had.

Oh, God. Will I ever get to sleep? I asked myself angrily as I started up out of another doze. The loges looked like the black holes graves make. They terrified me with their grim looks. I closed my eyes once more and fell into the same sort of heavy somnolence as before.

Suddenly!

What do I hear?

Steps. Yes. Steps. Quick, almost like leaping.

Can there be someone else in the auditorium? Who is it? I'm tired and weak. Maybe I'm dreaming.

I hear the movements again. Someone *is* jumping wildly, crazily over chairs. I sit up and try to see. There is a swift shadow moving, bowing, leaping in the dark with enormous speed.

Dear Lord in Heaven, who can it be? Someone? Someone? If he's human, why is he moving so fast that I can hardly see his shadow?

It's dark. Scary and dark.

The town clock strikes two: *Ding . . . dong.* Its echo resounds through the three stories of the auditorium. The lean black shadow disappears into a corner somewhere on the right. Now I can't even doze. Fear has entirely driven sleep away. My head aches and I am short of breath.

Who can it be? Who?

Is he human? Then why does he jump so wildly? So madly? What's he doing here in the middle of the night?

It's silent. Preternaturally still. Not a sound. Not a rustle. The dense silence expands on all sides and enfolds me in it. Terror seizes me. I turn my head. I strain my ears. I listen intently. Silence. Then . . . Yes. I hear something. Clearly.

Thump. Thump. It's the beating of a human heart. Whose? Perhaps it's my own. How can I possibly be hearing someone else's heart?

It's not my heart. It's the sound of someone else's.

I get up quickly from my chairs. I want to run away. Then I remember that the doors are locked, and I lie down again, over-whelmed. The pace of the sound increases. Every nook and cranny of my soul is invaded by fear. All of a sudden—I don't know how it comes to me—I have an inkling of what's happening.

Fire! There'll be a fire tonight.

Run! Quickly, save yourself. The devil himself has trapped you in a locked circus so that you'll die in the midst of flames. You're going to be burned to a crisp. Save yourself. The place will burn. My head is jangling. I hear noises, yells, cries. The wringing of hands. The sound of trumpets. Fiery red tongues quiver before my eyes. A conflagration. The circus is burning.

Suddenly it all vanishes. It's quiet again. Silent as before.

"Ha, ha, ha." I laugh because the nightmares are over. I breathe calmly again and stretch out my tall length on my bed of three chairs. So I made a fool of myself. Dear God, how childish I've become. How easily frightened—how superstitious. What an idiotic thing to suppose: that there's someone else in the auditorium. What conflagration? Nonsense. Pure imagination. I'm furious at myself.

Sleep, I tell myself. *Sleep, miserable creature. Consider yourself lucky that you don't have to sleep in the streets.*

I try my best to get to sleep, but no luck. I begin to feel sorry for myself. For the way—and for the frequency—with which I have been hard on myself. I feel tears creeping into my eyes. Self-pitying tears. I think, *Ah, brother, why do you revile yourself? It won't always be this way. It's a waste of tears. You're no worse than anyone else. Not by a hairsbreadth. Aren't you willing to do any kind of work at all? Then who's to blame you? Forgive me, brother, forgive me. You'll see, you'll be rewarded for all your grief.*

I feel better. I begin to doze off. The clock in the bell tower strikes 2:30. I wonder whether I'm asleep or not. No. I'm in a waking doze. My eyes are shut. My whole body is leaden with fatigue.

I'm not cold anymore. My faithful old coat keeps me warm.

I'm happy with it. I begin to weave a strange meditation around my coat. Let us imagine that I have money. A lot of money. So much that I can afford to buy a new coat. One with two rows of ivory buttons. Isn't it certain that then I would give my old coat to a rag dealer? Who else would think it had any value? No doubt about it, I would get rid of it. This very coat which is now keeping me warm would be rotting away somewhere. This coat, which has never been as loyal to me as it is now.

Oh, Lord God, how true and just is the world you've made. Nothing you have created is useless.

My head ached. I was hot. My whole body was feverish.

Thoughts, like gleaming sparks, flew through my mind. Swiftly, hurriedly, I reviewed all my experiences on the battlefields. The raw, bloody images wound themselves together to form a cluster that I recognized as my memories.

Suddenly one of the bloodiest of those battlefield events appeared before my eyes enveloped in the frightful veil of truth and experience.

13

For two months, enfolded from head to foot in crusted, freezing snow, we lay in the trenches on the Polish-Bolshevik front in White Russia. We lay about sleepily, suffering from fatigue, immobility, lassitude, and inertia. Looking up at the sky, we saw the sun rise day after day; and day after day it went down on the cheerless white snow-and ice-gripped fields and steppes.

Bored out of our minds with nothing to do, we peered over our trenches at the thin-legged, black-beaked crows that stood on the ground above us, pecking, tapping away at the food we had thrown out of the trenches. They aimed their sly, sharp glances at us and waited. Waited for something. Always waiting, never leaving us.

Each of the soldiers had his own crow, his personal guardian. Strange. Occasionally it would flap its black wings, rise into the cold air, and caw something to the snowbound fields. Then it flew off for a moment, only to return at once to its former place, where it resumed its waiting.

No one can imagine the horror of such a guardian. Day in and day out, sunrise after sunrise, always the crow with its black, pointed beak and its sly, small, treacherous black eyes. A crow as guardian—a secret, bizarre, false guardian of death.

I had lived for many years in a village, but I had never heard, not even from the wisest old peasants, that a crow could attach itself to someone whom it would refuse to leave.

I am a pale, anemic, fearful sort of person. Until I was fourteen I believed in ghosts and devils. My mother used to dress me in white as a talisman to keep me from dying young, the way my departed brothers and sisters had. My father had warned me to avoid churches, crosses, and crows, and a hostility toward churches, crosses, and crows had seeped into my blood. When, as a child, I saw a boy draw a cross in the sand with a stick, I avoided him and did not speak to him for years.

The waiting of the nearby crows intensified a secret, incomprehensible dark terror in our souls. We were not afraid of death, but the crows terrified us.

The cold was sharp, searing. The air stabbed at us as if with the points of knives. If anyone spilled a bit of water, it turned instantly into ice. The sullen skies seemed armor-plated, and our voices rising in the air gave off a sharp metallic echo, as if they had struck walls of steel and concrete.

We prayed for action: attack, movement, struggle. Man-to-man combat. The blood in our veins turned leaden. The sounds of rifle fire poured like buckshot into our ears.

At last, one evening when darkness slid across the pale fields, a voice, drunk with blood lust, was heard in the trenches: "Attack, brothers. Hey! Hey! Attack!"

We climbed out of our holes. We ran and ran. Ran into the dark and saw nothing. There was a cannonade, and, from the sky, a flaming rain of artillery shells and exploding shrapnel poured into the night. The earth and air shuddered. We saw nothing. We ran.

Suddenly there danced before us some dark, squirming little men. Dolls which moment by moment grew taller. Then wild creatures with madness in their eyes and contorted, inflamed faces arrived. They carried gleaming bayonets between their clenched teeth. There were deafening cries. Daggers glittered. Artillery thundered and spat out gouts of fiery lava.

Then silence. Not a breath of air. Not a soul. No fire.

I can't remember what happened. I know only that when I woke I was lying on the ground. It was cold and dark. Blue snow and black night everywhere on field and steppe.

A dull pain tore at my left foot. As I looked around I saw several corpses with glazed eyes, but I was in pain and ignored them. I stumbled about, moving unsteadily, drunkenly over the frozen earth like a man who has been felled.

When I bent to take a good look at my foot, I saw that a plug of bloody, hardened flesh dangled from it, as if a great nail had been driven through the foot.

It was dark. Silent. I walked on for an hour. Two. Then I felt my strength leaving me. Any minute now I would fall to the ground. It was still searing cold, even colder than it had been by day. I went on, not knowing where. I bit my lips against the cold. I felt myself trembling. My teeth chattered. I tucked my numbed hands between my thighs and tried to warm them.

My voice sad, subdued, desperate, I called, "Hello. Who . . . Who . . . Hello. Who . . . Who?"

On that vast silent steppe neither man nor dog replied. Nobody stirred. Nothing breathed. Not a gleam, not a light from a settlement or a village or a hut anywhere that my eye fell. I dragged on, exhausted, fainting. My lips were dry, my mouth leathery.

If only I could warm myself. Oh, for a glowing coal, for a bit of warmth to melt my frozen blood. That's all I asked.

Another step or two and I would fall to the ground. My knees buckled; my body swayed.

Dear God, is there a city somewhere? A town?

But only the hard wintry darkness caressed my gaze, and the cold seared and burned as if it meant to penetrate my clothing, to lick my naked body with its cold steel tongues.

"A bit of warm water . . . The cold will drop me to the ground like a frozen bird from a tree. I'm falling . . . "

Then my feet tripped on something heavy and huge. I fell.

As a hungry infant senses the smell of its mother's breast in the dark, so now I sensed warmth. My groping fingers touched something silken, soft, and warm.

"Ah!" It was a cry of joy torn from my mouth, and I fell clumsily, like a beast, upon whatever the thing was as onto a soft warm lap. When I looked more closely, I saw that I lay on a large, exhausted Belgian draft horse. A mass of black-and-red congealed blood hung from the horse's half-open mouth. At its base the mass was a jagged lump of tangled hair, but at its tip it came to a sharp point, like a goatee. The thing looked like the three-cornered hat of an Assyrian king.

The horse was still alive, gasping for breath with its last strength. I pressed myself against it. Like a madman, I flung myself from one side of the horse to the other, sucking in its warmth, breathing it in through my mouth, through my nostrils.

The horse, feeling the weight of my body, uttered a weak, pathetic groan. I put my bloody, wounded foot under one of its limbs and pressed my frozen face against its warm belly and nestled against its hide.

But I was still cold. I thought I would die of the cold. Suddenly I had a wild thought that made me shudder. I shouted aloud with the mad joy of someone rescued from death. Leaping to my feet, I stepped a pace away from the horse. In the space of a single breath I had my carbine knife out and *whack!* Gritting my teeth, I plunged the knife into the horse's belly with all my strength.

"Ahhhhhhh." There was an abrupt whistling sound in the air. It was the choked, profoundly human cry of a life being cut short.

No. I cannot believe that a dying horse could scream with a voice as profoundly human as that. No. I don't believe it.

Perhaps it was I who cried out for the horse I had murdered. Perhaps it was I who uttered that scream for a dying creature that no longer had enough strength of its own to scream.

A spurt of thick warm blood gushed over me. A caressing warmth, soft and heavy, flowed over my fists—which still grasped the carbine knife. The warmth flowed over my chest, my face, my neck. With the relentless tenacity of a predatory beast, with my last strength, with my hands, with my whole body I tore at the horse's belly till I had ripped its entrails out.

A red darkness blinded me. The horse's blood turned the night red. But then, I had no idea what sort of stuff blood can be. I cut and tore and plucked at the horse's entrails, flinging them aside.

Time passed.

I was covered with a cold sweat and soaked with blood. Finally the body was empty. I jumped for joy; then, squeezing myself together on the ground beside the horse, I crawled into its belly.

I was warm. Wonderfully warm. I was comfortable in the horse's huge roomy belly. I turned wearily over on my side and fell instantly into a deep sleep.

When I woke, the sun, like an alert soldier standing watch over a newly conquered land, stood in the eastern portion of the cold sky.

As I tried to climb out of the horse's belly, I sensed a certain heaviness—as if I were stuck to the inner walls of the creature's body. I made a convulsive movement and broke free.

A cold, sharp, biting wind together with a strange searing cold embraced me as in arms of steel. The cold immobilized me. I could not take a step. I spread my arms out only to see the most horrid thing imaginable. I was frozen to the earth. From head to foot I was enclosed in a Bordeaux-colored armor. I could not drop my arms. They stayed outstretched. My feet were stuck fast to the ground. I looked like a cross.

My God, I was rooted to the earth like a bloody red cross.

I was a bloody cross on the White Russian steppe.

It was frightful. Terrifying. Uncanny. I stood in an empty field where there was no sign of human life, no trace of a habitation. I stood, a frozen, human-shaped red cross.

I tried to shout and could not; to weep, but I could not. I felt how the bloody cross that imprisoned me, that rooted me like a tree to the earth, gnawed slowly at my life.

Near me, to one side, lay the dead horse with its ripped-up belly from which protruded my hat, covered with frozen blood. On the other side lay the creature's ripped-out heart, lungs, and intestines, all of them covered with silvery frost as by a winding sheet. Between the hat and the entrails I stood—a living bloody cross.

How was it that I, who as a child could never stand to watch my friends torturing a cat—how could I have cut open the belly of a living horse with my own hands?

The horse's blood shrieked accusations at my body. It tortured me. It choked me. It sucked my breath.

I tried to move and could not. I stood welded in place.

"Ohhhh," I wailed like a child who tries to walk but cannot. I stood in the empty waste like a frozen tombstone with the cross of myself upon it.

All at once the glazed eyes of the murdered horse acquired life and laughed at me. "Ah, humanity."

My head throbbed. I could no longer hear, and then before my eyes the day's brightness turned into a mixture of darkness, dizzying pallor, and blood.

I dozed off. It grew dark. Night became the entire world—enormous, profound, velvety night. My eyes grew heavy. My doze began to rock me to sleep.

With the last strength of a dying man, I shook my arms—and I achieved my desire: the cross broke. My arms were free. Then, with the remnant of my waning strength, I began to beat my body everywhere. I slapped my cheeks, beat my chest, my head. And the bloody ice broke everywhere on me, like shards.

Finally I was entirely free. I was no longer a cross.

The horse, with its sardonic congealed eyes, watched me beat at my body, punishing myself. Driven by some interior force, I dropped to my knees beside it and prayed for forgiveness. I wept. I yelled. I tore the hair, the bloody hair from my head.

14

I kept my eyes closed and was beginning to feel that I was falling asleep. Suddenly I felt a stream of blazing light through my closed eyelids. Startled, I raised my head.

What do I see?

Am I dreaming, or is this dazzle from a weakened, addled brain? No, I'm not dreaming.

All the ceiling lights in the huge circus auditorium are on. I get off my makeshift couch and kneel, my hands pressed against the near wall of the loge. The clock in the tower strikes three.

In the arena of the brightly lighted, deserted circus there is a man standing on a sort of high podium. His face is pale, translucent; his eyes are large and feverish; his hair is black and disheveled. He has a sheet of paper in his hands. I hear his deep voice as he reads, "My Song to No One."

His face is unnaturally white, as if a corpse were standing at midnight in a circus ring declaiming poetry. I can tell his knees are trembling, his hands are shaking. His pointed chin makes his elongated face resemble a triangle, and the look in his face is a blend of sleepiness and sickly inspiration.

Now I begin to understand that the footsteps I heard were his.

Who is he? A madman? A nightwalker? What's he doing in the circus at this hour?

"Oh." His large dark eyes have caught sight of my head in the first-floor loges, and for a moment he is distracted from the long sheet of paper in his hand and looks about. He panics and stands stunned, not knowing what to do, as if he were thinking, "Shall I run or stand still?" Then, turning to me, he says tensely, "Who are you?"

Without answering his question, I make an attempt at an

apology: "I'm sorry if my being here has disturbed you." I repress an impulse to smile. "You seem to be a poet."

Angrily, suspiciously, he says, "I'm not a poet."

"And yet you are reading a poem."

"Yes, I was reading one, but it isn't mine," he says insultingly, his eyes continuing to shine.

"Whose?"

"Ah, whose? Even if I told you whose it was, would you recognize the name? What do you know about such things?" he says contemptuously. His angular features are contorted.

"As a matter of fact, I do know something."

"You know something. Ha, ha." It is a scornful, a painful laugh. "You know some. . . Well, since you know something about such things, I'll tell you. The poem is by the brilliant and famous poet Vogelnest." The words provoke him to laughter again.

I shrug. "I don't know any famous Polish poet named Vogelnest."

"You don't know him?" He is incensed, and a flush spreads over his face. "That doesn't mean that there is no such poet. Take a good look. The man himself is standing before you. Viktor Vogelnest, one of the brightest stars in the firmament of poetry. You understand," he adds, "that I am such a star in the world of poetry that I am kept in a jewel case—so my light will not shine." His laugh is bitter, painful.

His Polish pronunciation was beautiful. In his angular features one could see, despite his affectation of witty indifference, signs of depression and grief. There were indications, too, that he had an instinctive ability to understand complex human qualities. In his eyes, his truly Jewish, misty, dark eyes, shadowed by his brows, tiny lights played. As he watched me, his look was at first penetrating, sly, almost contemptuous, as if he meant in that single glance to understand me, to know who and what I was. Then it became attentive, dignified, as if saying, "Respect me." One could read a trace of nobility, too, in his long, thin Jewish nose, All in all, his was a strange and expressive face in which was mirrored a complex and suffering soul.

His joke about himself as a star in the poetic firmament was told without a smile—as I could tell because he was at no great distance from me and because the circus was so brightly lighted. It was also clear to me that he understood exactly what he was saying. Perhaps he regarded me with derision because he thought I was capable of understanding only the simplest meaning of his words. Probably.

"What are you doing here?" he asked again and waited, like a keen-eyed policeman preparing himself to probe the truth of my answer.

"I've no place else to sleep."

"You've come here to sleep?"

"Yes."

"Who gave you permission?"

"Nobody."

His hostility, I noticed, was perceptibly diminishing; there was even a trace of friendliness in his face.

For a while he stood musing. Then he gave a short, nervous laugh, which sounded strange and frightening in the empty auditorium of the circus. With sly servility, he said, "You think I'm crazy?"

"No," I replied.

" 'No,' you say. Then you don't know much about people."

I was amazed at his candor and studied him more closely. I continued to see imprinted in his face traces of slyness, humor, and misery. And it was easy to suspect that he might be deceiving me for some secret purpose.

"No," he went on. "You choose not to understand me." He drew back, though his eyes continued to glow ardently. "Furthermore, you're not telling the truth. Mind you, I'm contemptuous of your truth," he sneered. "I know that a man who reads his poems in an empty circus at midnight is crazy."

Silently I lowered my head. The movement made my hat fall over the loge rail.

"Wait, I'll bring it up to you." A moment or two later he was in the loge with me. Now I could get a close look at him. The shadows from the baseboard of the loge gave an even sharper look to his features. His legs trembled. He flung his head about. His weird movements gave me considerable anxiety. He had the look of a drunk.

Again he studied me, this time very intently. A few moments passed in silence, after which he put out his hand. I took it, and he pressed my hand firmly, then let it go. With a certain pleading earnestness he said, "You're a decent person. If you weren't, you wouldn't be dressed as you are, or be sleeping here. I'd like to be your friend, because people like you are alone in the world, and so am I.

"You're perplexed when you look at me. You can't figure me out. No question but that you think I'm mad. Or at least drunk. To sneak into a theater at midnight—that would occur only to a disordered mind." He smiled. "Do you know that your hand is very hot?" As if suddenly coming to himself, he changed his tone. "You've got a fever . . . you're not well. Look how strangely you stare at me.

"You know, there are times when I turn as restless as a thunderstorm and seem to feel the earth trembling at my feet. At such moments I see what a ridiculous, what a foolish role I play in the world. At such soul-searing times I hear an inner voice that says, 'Go, find a deep, dense forest, and there scream at the top of your voice. Scream! Scream until you've deafened yourself.'"

He paused briefly, his head lowered, like one condemned, after which he began again. Only he was calmer, calmer now. "For the last several weeks I have been tormented by a feeling that I had to read my poems—which no one is willing to publish. That I had to read them in an auditorium at night. I wanted to shout them out in an empty theater. I was shaken by the idea when it occurred to me. How beautiful, how glorious it was!" Here he expanded his chest and stood without moving for a few seconds.

Suddenly he shook my hand and started off without a word. He looked pale, exhausted, as if he had had a seizure of apathy. Then he resumed his earlier sly, ironic manner and said, "And you really don't think I've been talking nonsense?"

Puzzled, I looked intently at him. "I can't say that I understand you."

He ran off, laughing.

The lights went out. I fell asleep.

15

It was nine o'clock in the morning—I could tell from the sound of the tower clock that echoed loudly in the empty circus. I got up and started pacing back and forth, both to warm up and to stretch my legs. Out of sheer boredom I found myself counting my paces: fifteen, sixteen, seventeen. I wondered when anyone would come to open the circus doors. Some time passed this way, with me counting my steps. The place was still pitch dark because there was no window anywhere through which a bit of daylight might peep in. One might have thought it was night. *How many paces can one make in an hour?* I asked myself, for no better reason than to have something to think about.

Eight hundred and two.

Why eight hundred and two? Why eight hundred and two exactly?

I laughed at the stubborn way in which I clung to the idea of eight hundred and two. Then I heard someone passing by.

Have they opened the circus? Are people here?

Aha! Someone has come into the loge where I am. Pitch dark as it is, I sense that it is Vogelnest.

"Maybe you can tell me whether the night is over?" he asks wearily, rumpling the thick locks of his black hair.

"It's long past daybreak."

"How do you know?"

"I heard the striking of the clock in the tower."

"Then you know what time it is?"

"Yes, it's after nine. Maybe nine thirty."

"They won't come to open the place till eleven. Until then there's no way out." He seated himself on a chair. In the dark his eyes had a restless, angry gleam. He sat thus beside me for some fifteen minutes without speaking a word.

"How long have you been sleeping in the circus?" I inquired.

He stamped his foot furiously. "I beg you, let me be quiet until eleven o'clock." He seemed to swell like a sack and kept still. I watched him. He sat in a crouch, and his eyes seemed to be stalking something. But he did not keep silent until eleven. After sitting still for fifteen minutes, he struck the arm of his chair with a fist. Then, his voice desperate, mournful, trembling, he said, "To hell with me. I'm good for absolutely nothing. Absolutely useless. What stupidity I've pulled off tonight!" He turned toward me. "To read a poem in an empty circus—before no one! What madness! What idiocy! Ah, I've been sinking into a sea of such foolish impulses. Every day more and more. I wanted to give myself some sort of penance, and this is it: to say nothing until eleven o'clock in the morning. If you had any idea how much I love to talk, you'd understand the severity of such a penance."

Even in the dark, I could tell there was a twisted smile on his face.

What a strange fellow. I simply could not tell whether he was joking or whether he was being entirely serious. Abruptly he changed the manner of his speech and asked, "You wanted to know how long it's been since I've taken to sleeping here, isn't that right? Well, my friend, the first time—is the last time. I have a wife . . . a home."

"You're married?" I interrupted. I was surprised. "But last night you said you were all alone in the world."

"What I said . . . yes, it's what I said. And what I said is true."

He came close, took my hand, and squeezed it. Tears glistened in his eyes.

I was astonished . . . confused. Who was he? What did he want? No, I was a long way from understanding him. I had not the slightest clue.

"You'll come with me today. You'll see my wife," he went on. I did not refuse.

He passed his hand frequently through his hair.

"It seems strange to you that I have a wife? That's something you didn't expect?" Again he smiled and was still.

Then he spoke again in his hasty fashion, spewing his words as if he could not bear to keep them in, as if he were choking on them. He mixed things up, linking together matters that had nothing to do with each other. Speech gushed from him. Then abruptly he stopped. Exhausted. Overcome by a great weariness, he flung himself into a chair, as if he were a mass of dead flesh, and was still.

At ten thirty the circus was opened. Several acrobats came in, then a stagehand, and then Doli, the clown. One of the acrobats was very fat; he moved with difficulty, panting. The stagehand wheeled out a wagon full of heavy weights. Doli, dressed in a black suit and wearing lacquered pumps, danced in the arena and swung his stick about, muttering angrily, "To the royal executioner with them—waking me at nine thirty. My eyes are still stuck together."

"Ha, ha," laughed the heavy acrobat, his eyes so hidden by his plump lids that they almost disappeared. "Sleep's good for you, Doli. When you're asleep, you don't know you're a Lilliputian."

Tiny, sleepy Doli was outraged. "Sleep's even better for you. When you're asleep, you don't know you're a cow."

The acrobats laughed. One of them caught Doli up and set him, trembling, on his shoulder. Doli bit his lip and said nothing: not because Doli the clown was afraid—he had his own brand of heroism and fought back with all his might—but because wit was his weapon. "You should have carried me about like this long ago. Considering how long you've been a jackass, I might have been riding you all along."

The insult worked. He was set down on the ground. Those

muscle-bound creatures had not the least notion how to deal with Doli the clown.

Tiny Doli delighted me. I wanted to hang around, to see what else was likely to happen, but Vogelnest tugged at my sleeve. We walked out of the circus.

16

It was raining. The streets were covered with mud, and there was a whipping, aggressive wind that was determined to topple down walls. It wept, howled, shrieked, and plucked at our ears. I turned up my collar and kept moving. Vogelnest, immersed in thought, said nothing. He spat from side to side and whispered silent curses. The rain lashed his tense face, which seemed to turn paler, bonier. All at once there was a small crowd before us. A tramway stopped; its passengers descended and, clustering together, joined the crowd. Vogelnest and I approached. A dog had been run over. The paving stones, the rails, and the tram's wheels were splattered with blood, which the rain was rapidly washing away.

The dog's head and one foot had been severed from its body and lay some distance away. People talked, gesticulated, shouted. The motorman made excuses for himself and held something up for everyone to see. Vogelnest, seeing the dog's mutilated body, trembled. I could hear his teeth chattering.

He started off, taking long strides as if running away.

"Come along. Hurry." He tugged at my sleeve. We were moving very quickly. I heard Vogelnest say, "The poor dog."

Vogelnest was still as pale as death. Then he started to talk, his speech angry, fragmented. "Dogs. That's all we need in this world. That's all this rubbish heap needs. Dogs." From the tone of his speech it was clear that he had thought about the matter. "There isn't a wise man in Europe who can explain why dogs had to be created. I can't begin to understand it. Ah, Lord, Your world is so idiotic." He bowed his head in despair.

Vogelnest looked so sad it was funny.

We turned into a narrow street. Tall slender houses, with tiny windows like eyes, stared at each other. Workers' houses, in two straight lines, looked up at Heaven with hostility, as if they had sworn to block the sun. And in fact the street was muddy and dark, as if lassitude itself were sprawled on the roofs on both sides of the street. One could readily say, "There is no sky here."

We climbed up to the fifth story of one of the houses. Vogelnest opened a door, and we went into a small room where a woman sat at a table, sewing something. She looked up at us with brown, intelligent eyes in which there was a nearly imperceptible, delicate sorrow. She did not ask Vogelnest where he had been but put her sewing to one side, stood up, and poured us two mugs of hot coffee. She took a loaf of bread from a cupboard, then sugar and butter, and set them before us on the table.

"Will you eat?" she inquired, her voice soft and melancholy.

"Yes, of course we'll eat," Vogelnest replied and clapped me affectionately on the shoulder. "You won't refuse, right?"

I drank the hot coffee with pleasure. As I drank, I stole glances at the woman. I wondered why she did not ask where her husband had been all night. Had he perhaps told her where he meant to go? No, that was impossible. She would have kept him from doing anything that crazy.

She was short, but not extremely so. Her oval face was pale, her lips soft and full, with pronounced dimples at the corners. There was an instinctive childlike sweetness in her soft young lips. Her cheeks had a slightly sallow cast, and there was an unhealthy red tinge at her cheekbones—a clear sign of tuberculosis. Her brown eyes were large, intelligent, sad, and kind. Her long chestnut hair fell down past her slender pale throat. She wore a clean yellow muslin dress, and an equally clean batiste blouse and a pair of step-in house slippers. Everything about her spoke of fatigue and breathed sorrow. She was as gentle and quiet as a dove. And sparing in her speech. The deep blue circles under her eyes betrayed a severe nervousness which, just then, she tried to hide.

I could not keep from staring at her. Then all at once I noticed that there were broad streaks of gray in her chestnut hair. No, not gray—actually white hair.

She caught my glance, and the red spots in her cheeks became more visible. She was a bit unsettled and turned her large eyes away from my bold gaze.

She stood. "Perhaps you'll have a bit more coffee?" she asked in a gentle pleasant voice that had in it a strange servility that absolutely startled me.

"No need to ask us, Clara. Give us a couple of cups and we'll drink," Vogelnest said, not even turning to her.

Quietly she went over to the small pot and poured two more cups of coffee. I began to drink my second cup. Vogelnest grew drowsy. His head fell forward onto the table and he went off into a doze. Clara, his wife, came up and, in the tone of a devoted mother, inquired, "Viktor, are you sleepy? Then get into bed. Your friend will excuse you." She turned toward me with a gentle smile on her intelligent face. I nodded. She removed his shoes and his upper clothing, and Vogelnest lay down in the only clean bed and promptly fell asleep.

I was getting good and warm. I felt my whole body turning hot. The rain drummed at the shutters, and the windowpanes made uncanny sounds. Clara sat down and resumed her sewing. The slender fingers of her pale beautiful hands moved skillfully. I felt grateful to her, and it occurred to me to thank her by telling her—something. Something intimate, personal, such as women enjoy hearing. But I could not think of a way to begin. So I kept still and looked at her poignant, lovely face, at her slender white hands. Then she raised her large eyes to mine and said shyly, "I gather that you've served in the army."

"Yes."

"And you've been discharged?"

"Yes. It's three weeks since I became a civilian."

"Do you have a job?"

"No. Before I was drafted, I used to work for a firm. But it closed down."

"Then you're not doing anything?" she asked sympathetically.

"No. I'm not doing anything."

"It must be very hard on you."

"One does what one can. It's not hopeless."

She was silent, her eyes lowered. "You look scruffy enough to frighten people. Maybe you'd like to wash up?"

"Thanks so much. I won't say no."

She got up and set a basin of warm water and some soap before me.

I took my hat off. Then, still wearing my coat, I started to wash. My sleeves got wet. When I raised my arms, filthy water dripped to the clean floor. I reddened with shame and regretted undertaking to wash, humiliated by the dirty water running down my face into the basin. I picked the basin up, and, hiding it with my body, started to go toward the stairs, meaning to descend to the courtyard, where I intended to empty the dirty water. I was blushing to the tips of my ears. Evidently she was aware of my distress, because she stood some distance away and pretended not to see the basin full of dirty water or the black droplets dripping from my sleeve onto the floor. I went down into the courtyard, emptied the water, and came back up. Still embarrassed, I sat down, my eyes lowered. I was terribly upset because of my helplessness. I felt that I had made the whole room filthy—the room kept neat and clean by the constant toil of her lovely hands. I felt absolutely at my wit's end. The trivial business of washing up pained me to the point of tears. And I'd fallen in love with this noble and good woman from the first moment I saw her. I, who was myself so depressed, so miserable.

I stuck the wet cuffs of my coat into my pockets to hide them and sat thinking that she was undoubtedly displeased. I had heard tales of how even an intelligent woman could be so irritated because a picture on a wall had been moved that she was prepared to do battle simply to get her way about how it should be hung. Suddenly, quite near me, I heard the sound of laughter and felt the motion of her breath. "You forgot to wipe your face." She tossed a white towel at my head. I turned an even brighter red and touched my face. It was wet. The breeze in the courtyard had only lightly dried it.

"Ha, ha, ha," I laughed. "I forgot. That's really clever of me." More confused than ever, I rubbed quickly at my face with the towel. The clock struck the hour. "It's twelve o'clock. I've got to go." I put the towel down, opened the door, and called a pathetic *"Adieu."* And without a word of thanks, I practically ran away.

On the staircase I paused for a while and thought. Then, when I had descended several steps to the first landing, I heard the hasty opening of a door. I turned and looked up. There in the doorway was Clara, powdered and painted. Even her eyelids had been darkened. I thought she was beautiful just then. Very beautiful. She stood looking down at me, her hands on her hips, and uttered a long peal of laughter. A woman's laughter.

I stood on the staircase, puzzled. *Is it really she?*

Yes.

I heard the latching of the door.

All the way back to the circus I wondered about her. What had she wanted of me? Perhaps she was a woman who enjoyed sinning with every man she could get?

I passed a store window with mirrors in it. The place attracted me, and I stopped to look at myself in the mirrors. My face was lean, bony, pale. I had grown a considerable beard. The long, wild hair of my head, from which dirty hanks stuck out, joined in a line with the beard. I studied my face intently in one of the mirrors and saw the effects of sleepless nights in my eyes. I was unnaturally pale, like someone who has just risen from a long and severe illness. My decrepitude and my torn soldier's coat with its raised collar made me look, to the most casual glance, like someone from another world.

I looked neither young nor old. No one could have guessed my age. My eyes seemed to have receded deep under my brows, and my cheekbones protruded. I was amazed at how lean, how emaciated my face was. I was overwhelmed with pity. *I look like a ghost.* I stared more intently into the mirror and felt my throat constrict. *The woman was making a fool of me. No doubt about it. She was ridiculing me.*

The door of the shop before whose window I was standing opened, and a stout man, a cigar in his mouth, came out. He turned rudely to me and, in the stern voice one uses to speak to inferiors, said, "This place isn't meant for people who want to preen in a mirror for hours on end."

His angry tone lashed at me like a whip. I stood where I was, readying myself for an imaginary battle. My face was contorted with anger. "I have a perfect right to look for as long as I like. I've been at the front for four years. Do you know what that means? Four years. I've been in battle on three fronts. Don't think I'm some kind of a bum. Before I was drafted, I was an accountant for Boritsky and Company, a well-known corporation. If you don't believe me, look at this!"

Hardly knowing what I did, I pulled an old torn document out of my pocket and threw it at him in the doorway. The document did indeed certify that I had worked in the main accounting office of Boritsky and Company. Having thrown the paper at him, I ran off like a windstorm.

When finally I slowed down, I wasn't far from the circus. Without knowing exactly why, I felt myself insulted and injured.

What I said to the mirror man was so stupid. Each day that goes by, I get stupider. I seem to keep falling butter-side down.

The heavy, dismal rain continued to fall. The wind tore unceasingly at street lamps and signs. There were few people in the streets. Only rarely did someone hurriedly pass me by.

The manager was already in the circus when I got there. He was in his office, pacing back and forth, making calculations.

"Today you'll carry the placard in the afternoon only. That old sign got soaked. I've ordered another one. Come this afternoon," he said. I waited silently for a moment.

The manager drew on his cigarette. "Ah, you want some money."

He pulled a few thousand marks from his pocket and tossed them to me. I went out into the street.

It was already as dark as evening. My shoes were filled with mud, and I was entirely rain soaked. I walked through a couple of narrow streets. The image of Vogelnest's wife was continually before me. Her fresh young lips. The depth of suffering in her eyes.

Dear Lord, how wonderful it would be to be near someone like her. How sweetly she treated me—a filthy, ragged fellow. And what's more, a stranger. My thoughts of her turned eerie, bizarre, fantastic. I imagined that she had been waiting for me for a long, long time. That she knew me from somewhere. Somewhere.

Then I remembered the sound of her laughter as she stood in the doorway. What was the meaning of that laughter? For whom had she dolled herself up that way? I had no idea.

There was a barbershop across the street. I went in and asked for a shave and a haircut. The white-smocked barber looked closely at me and hesitated. Evidently I didn't please him. He asked me to sit down and called his apprentice, whose usual task was to brush the customers' clothes.

"Shave the gentleman," the barber said and turned his back on me to keep his other customers from seeing my ragged coat through whose rents various bits of my filthy shirt peeped out.

When my hair was cut and I had been shaved, the boy said, "That will be two hundred marks for the boss." He nodded toward the man in the white smock.

I took a thousand-mark bill from my pocket and paid. I got eight hundred marks in change. "Here's a tip for you," I said, tossing the eight hundred marks to the boy. Turning on my heels, I left the shop.

I was some distance away from the barbershop when I heard a voice calling after me. "You've made a mistake. You gave the boy too much money." The man calling to me had the eight hundred marks in his hand.

I did not turn around but kept walking, playing over in my mind the scene in which the amazed apprentice counted out so much money in his hand, and imagining the astonishment of the man in the white smock.

I was pleased.

17

For several days in a row the manager of the Vangoli Circus was irritable and angry. He paced his office, spewing clouds of smoke from his thick smuggled German cigarettes, muttering, "Five or six thousand? That's a loss, damn it."

He did not reply to my greeting but strode back and forth, seeing no one.

Then, abruptly, he noticed me. "Do I owe you any money?"

"Yes, you do," I replied.

"How much?"

"Eight thousand marks."

He took several bills from a yellow leather billfold and handed them to me.

I started to leave. The manager gave me a penetrating look and said, "Wait a minute. I've something to discuss with you."

I paused on the threshold.

He went on. "Can you speak well?"

I smiled. "Well, I can speak."

"In Polish, too?"

"Yes, in Polish."

"I can help you to earn some money." He was silent for a second or two. Then, speaking more loudly, he said, "Let me explain. It's like this. I'm half-owner of the Venus Cinema, which is, as you know, in an entirely working-class neighborhood. Most of the workers can't read the screen titles. What I want you to do is this: as the film runs, you'll speak through a hole in the screen and tell them what they're seeing so they'll know what's happening. Do you get it? You'll have to speak loudly, clearly—and what you say will have to be interesting. In-ter-es-ting. They have to hear you, and they have to like what they hear. You have to speak boldly. You have to attract the audience so that they'll want to listen to you.

"Like this, for instance: on the screen, ten cops are in a battle with the bandit Zigomir. What you have to say is: 'In order to capture the great bandit king Zigomir, the Paris Prefecture of Police has sent out ten of its finest undercover agents. One of Zigomir's faithful henchmen brings him this news (which the henchman learned from a document stolen from a fireproof steel safe he cracked in the Prefecture of Police). Zigomir, hearing the report, smiles, takes out his revolver, points it toward the sky, and cries, "Ten is more than one, but I, Zigomir, king of the Black Skeleton Band, will know what to do with the treacherous scoundrels."'"

The manager altered his tone. "Do you understand? That's the way you have to talk. The audience hates cops; it loves bandits. To them, Zigomir is a god. They see Zigomir as powerful. Powerful. Ha, ha. At the moment when Zigomir raises his revolver, you have to say, 'Zigomir has prepared fifty rounds of dumdum ammunition. Forty-nine bullets for the cops closing in on him. One round to shatter his own courageous heart.' When Zigomir shoots, you don't merely say, 'Zigomir is shooting.' Rather, what you say is, 'Zigomir sends off a fusillade.' Or 'Zigomir is bombarding his foes.' When Zigomir has twenty rounds left, you announce that he has nineteen more shots before the final one. Victory or death. A heroic life or a lonely grave. That's the sort of lingo you have to speak. Get it? Do you want to try it? I can see you're an intelligent fellow. You ought to do it well."

"I think I can, yes," I replied.

"Good. Beginning tomorrow, you start on your new career. Tomorrow at six in the evening. Be at the Venus Cinema."

"Good! *Adieu*."

I went out into the street. The weavers were still on strike. Relaxed-looking workers wearing their Sunday clothes wandered about the town looking like people who have just been released from prison. They poked fun at every portly rich man who chanced to go by. Angry street insults, scathing remarks, venomous comments whizzed through the air.

One of the workers, a fellow with a wide mouth, embittered lips, and deep-set eyes in which there shone the cheerless glint of an alcoholic, stared boldly into the eyes of one such fat man who was approaching him and a couple of other workers. The laborer cried out, "See, brothers, he's stolen our bellies. Three-quarters of his belly belongs to us. We made that belly of his with our labor. If it weren't for us, he'd be thin as a spider. What use would he be to anyone, that good-for-nothing?" Then all three of the workers burst into wild laughter in which the echo of a piercing hatred could be heard.

The fat man who was being mocked pretended he had not heard the joke made at his expense, but his plump ears—like buttons made of flesh—trembled as he quickened his pace.

Newsboys ran about waving their papers and shouting, "Director Zavadsky Yields Five Percent More!"

The newsboys selling the evening papers moved with such speed it almost seemed that they had been shot from the editorial offices and, unable to bring themselves to a stop, had to keep on with their flight through the town.

"Ha, ha. He's getting smarter, Director Zavadsky," said someone in a cluster of men on a street corner. "He's already willing to add five percent. It's not enough. No. Even half a percent less than thirty-five will be too little. We've starved long enough. Let them yield."

"They could give one hundred percent, if only they wanted to," said a thin woman with a withered face who breathed quickly, hoarsely through her open mouth.

There was noisy activity everywhere in the streets. Workers milled about on all sides; and wherever one went, one heard, "Five percent," "Director Zavadsky," and "Strike."

I went into a small restaurant and had something to eat. Then I went back out into the street. The sun was bright without giving warmth. Such heat as its rays gave was sucked up by the pale wintry chill that surged through the town. I thought about Vogelnest and his wife and was utterly unable to understand them. I knew nothing about them—what sort of work they did, how they got their livelihood. Though I racked my brain thinking about them, I was not one bit the wiser.

I strolled about this way until evening; then I went back to the circus.

The auditorium was sparsely filled, except for the galleries, which were crowded with workers. Around ten o'clock, as the performance was coming to a close, I went out into the street again. The wrestler, Jason, walked out with me. Jason was the one who was billed as "The Latvian Champion." He was the audience's darling. He had a genteel, silken smile. When he bowed deftly before the crowd, he seemed to be as delighted as a child. He was a very handsome man, muscular but supple as a cat. His eyes were large, candid, and glowed with friendly *joie de vivre*. He pleased audiences because of the way he treated the opponents over whom he triumphed. After he pinned them to the mat, he would help them up; then, his arms around their shoulders, he walked with them around the arena in the friendliest fashion. He often gave them chocolate bars.

Turning to me, he said, "Come into town with me for a while." He knew me as a circus "hand." He took my arm in a comradely way, and we went off together.

"You're a Pole?" he asked, smiling, looking intently at me with his intelligent brown eyes.

"No. I'm a Jew."

"Well, in that case, *shalom aleichem*." He shook my hand.

"You're also a Jew?" I said, surprised.

"There are all sorts. I'm a real Jew from Latvia."

"No one would ever take you for a Jew. There's nothing the least bit Jewish about your appearance. You look like a true Gentile," I said.

"So?" he said. Arm in arm with him, I could feel the steely power of his tremendous body. "You're right. How does a Jew get to be an athlete and, on top of that, make a living from his muscles as well? But let's not talk about that. Believe me, my profession still revolts me. Come on, let's go into a tavern. I love low-class bars where there are drunks rolling about like corpses and where one drinks from a bottle and not from a glass."

As he spoke, the wild look of a street urchin came into his eyes. "I love the dives, but not because of their poverty. You've got it wrong if that's what you think."

He stood musing, gazing off into the distance, past the noise and bustle of the street. I understood how he felt and was drawn to him. For five minutes or so he said nothing. Then he began: "The Gentile world takes me for a Gentile. It's really very funny. My father was a pious, respectable Jew. He certainly never imagined he'd have the kind of son that I am. A fellow who wanders about the world with a circus."

There was a bitter twist to his full, red lips.

We turned down a quiet street where there were no street lamps burning. It was dark. There was no one to be seen anywhere. There were gloomy red gleams of light in the windows we passed. As we went farther down this lane where night seemed to have settled down comfortably like sleeping livestock, we heard the sounds of a cheap violin and a barrel organ. Jason lighted a match by whose light we made out a shop on whose doors were affixed various metal signs. Above two of the doors there was a sign that read, CARLOS BAR, OWNER: VLADISLAV SHUBRAK.

We opened the door and went in. The "bar" was in deep shadow. There was no electric light. Two kerosene lamps with long shades spread a reluctant illumination. A sickly, surly, sallow-faced Gentile with glazed, deep-set eyes stood under a broken yellow balustrade. He hardly moved and looked like a statue of a morbid, sleepy old man. The ceiling was held up by a wooden post set in the middle of the room. There were thick nails driven into the post on which clothes were meant to be hung. A young man with a fiddle and an older fellow with a barrel organ leaned against the post. The younger man wore a patched jacket under which a yellow knit shirt with black stripes could be seen. He wore thick sports socks, which, here and there, were filthy and torn—a sign, of course, that he too was an artist. The second man turned the handle of the barrel organ in a mechanical, bored, almost unwilling way. There was a glass of beer set on top of the barrel organ, from which, at frequent intervals, his eyes dreamily closed, he drank. He had the sunburned, wind-whipped look of a wandering village minstrel. Both musicians leaned against the post as if they had been condemned to play.

The bar was narrow but very long. And where the illumination in the place seemed to end, there were wooden tables and chairs. Voices, drunk or half-drunk, pressed toward the door as if they meant to break out into the street. The place was enveloped in a haze composed of alcohol, the smell of salty snacks, and stinking human odors—a haze so thick it almost completely shut out the light from the two kerosene lamps. Every so often a confused drunken voice was heard in the dark bar commanding stupidly, "Hey, musicians, play a tango."

"The Zigomir Waltz," came another more aggressively drunken voice straining to be heard above the others.

The musicians paid no attention to any of the requests. They dozed on, fixed in place like prisoners, playing whatever their hands might choose.

Then wobbly footsteps were heard. From the bar's darkest depths now emerged into the feeble light a disheveled droshky driver, his coat unbuttoned. His beefy wrinkled face was covered with sweat, and there was a melancholy, foggy look in his tiny eyes. He looked like a horse fresh from the manure smells of his stall. He went up to the musicians and punched them lightly in the stomach.

"Sons of bitches, why don't you play what you're told?" The musicians clutched their bellies, then, with sly humility, asked, "What shall we play?"

"A tango!" shouted the droshky driver angrily, like an officer whose command is not being obeyed.

"We can't play the tango if we're hungry."

"You can't? You have to!" the droshky driver shouted. "That's what you're paid for."

"Paid? Who's paying us?" they contradicted.

"Shubrak is."

"Ha, ha. Him!" They pointed at the old man leaning against the balustrade. "It'll be easier to eat the barrel organ and the fiddle than to get a groschen out of Shubrak."

The driver took several coins from his pocket and tossed them to the musicians, who caught them with the skill of beggars catching alms. They began to play a tango. The driver smiled drunkenly and again punched the musicians in the stomach and went back to his place.

Jason's face glowed with pleasure. "Remarkable. I love this place," he murmured. We sat down at a table in the front half of the bar. A slim young Gentile with a thick head of blond hair and a strained look in his shifty bright eyes hurried over to us on thin rachitic legs.

"What will the gentlemen have?"

"Spirits," Jason said.

"A bottle?"

"A bottle."

Then the young man started to laugh—a repressed, secretive laugh. His face flushed, and he broke out into a sweat. Then he winked, like someone sharing a secret. "*Proshe bardso*. Please," he said with elaborate respect, after which he ran off on his thin legs only to return at once with a bottle of spirits. He wiped off the table. Fascinated, his eyes fixed on Jason, he set the bottle down before us courteously.

It was noisy in the bar. Drunken voices mingled with the clink of glassware and the sound of the fiddle and the barrel organ. The old man at the buffet continued to stand rigid and immovable as a statue, but his eyes seemed to be silently flirting with a picture on the opposite wall, a picture of a stout healthy peasant woman with well-covered large breasts and a flushed face who held a mug of beer in her hand.

Jason poured two glasses of whiskey. We drank them down.

"You must understand." He puffed on his cigarette as he began. "Here, among you, my name is Jason. You may take it from me that it's not a name I chose for myself. My promoter gives me a different name in every country I go to. God forbid that I should need to remember all the names I've had. In Poland I'm a Latvian; in Latvia, a Pole. In Germany I'm a Belgian; in Belgium I'm a German." His laugh was open, hearty, healthy.

"From the time I was thirteen, I wandered about the world this way," he went on. "My father apprenticed me to a workingman, but I didn't want to leave my dogs behind, or give up my free life. After three weeks with my master, I ran away. I traveled on foot, hundreds of versts into the Russian interior. I slept in peasant huts. In Moscow some rich woman picked me up. I lived with her a full three years. She taught me Russian and fed me like a count. I was the apple of her eye; she wouldn't leave me alone for a moment. I ran away from her, taking with me three hundred rubles I'd saved out of the pocket money she gave me each day. I took off and went wherever my eyes—or my footsteps—led me.

"In Bessarabia I crossed the Romanian frontier. And it was in Romania, in the first town on the other side of the border, that a street urchin betrayed me to the police. I was arrested and sent to prison. I was nineteen years old. Healthy and strong as a whale.

"The prison director's wife, a young and beautiful Hungarian, cast her eye on me and persuaded her husband to let me be a household servant. There then began for me days of intoxication and love. My mistress's husband, in addition to being a drunkard, was perpetually busy. He had business in the capital city and was in Bucharest practically every other day. And all that while the beautiful Hungarian plied me with wine and held me an absolute captive in her continually feverish arms. She confided to me that she detested her husband because he had a fondness for handsome young men. She swore that she loved me and begged me often to run away with her to Russia or to Hungary. She had plenty of money, she said, and promised that we could afford to live happily for the rest of our lives. There were tears in her glowing dark eyes when she talked of her husband, and hatred compressed her beautiful soft red lips. I believed she was telling the truth.

"In general, her husband was not a bad fellow, and by day he treated her quite well and she could usually have her way with him. But often at night as I lay in my bed in one of the front rooms, I could hear the sound of repressed weeping. I listened closely, and I knew it was she, Ella, the Hungarian.

"In the morning I asked her what had happened. She lowered her eyes and, instead of replying, said, 'Let's run away. I can't take it anymore.' She drew away from me, and it was clear to me that her husband beat her at night. My heart went out to her and we agreed to run off to Hungary.

"In addition to the passion Ella had enkindled in me, her Romanian husband disgusted me. Two days later he traveled once more to Bucharest. Ella told me that his trips were not really on business, that he went so he could disport himself in certain revolting houses of prostitution there.

"One day I was in the courtyard, working in the garden among the grapevines, thinking of home, of our plan to run off, of a thousand other things. Ella came close and, putting her pale frightened face against mine, she said, 'Now!'

"I understood that it was time for flight. She took plenty of money and jewelry. 'It's not stealing,' she explained. 'And the police can't do anything about it. My father's very rich. The dowry he gave with me amounts to ten times as much as I'm taking.'

"We agreed to go to Hungary, where it would be easier to cross the border. It did not take us long to get there, and we crossed over quickly. We spent a few days in Budapest. I got identity papers in the name of Khorvath and she was listed as my wife. That was the first time I used a name that was not my own: Sivo Kirbit Khorvath. Ella taught me Hungarian, and we settled down to get used to the country. I went about dressed in satins and silks, with nothing to do all day but to love Ella. But it was dangerous to stay too long in Budapest. Ella's husband, the Romanian, might very well come to the capital searching for us. We moved therefore to Tokaj, a small town in the Hungarian Carpathian Mountains where we rented a wonderful house in which we lived in peace and quiet—a life of love and wine. Did Ella really love me, you wonder? I never, either then or now, had the slightest doubt. Did I love her? Yes, I loved her, too. She was a sweet good creature. Perhaps she was not one of those lovers whose death leaves a lifelong wound. But she was the kind of woman who can give a special beauty, a unique savor to life. To this day I remember the period when I loved Ella as the most beautiful time of my life. We lived in a majestic region. Mountains one or two thousand meters high. Ancient forests. And the vivacious Ella beside me.

"But our idyll did not last very long. Our Garden of Eden time ended abruptly, and it was our own fault.

"We had changed our Romanian paper and gold money into Hungarian kroner—what would have been the point of carrying Romanian money with us? But just then the Communist revolution erupted. Bela Kuhn became the dictator of Hungary. The value of Hungarian money was wiped out. The new regime, using hundreds of presses, printed new money which it disseminated throughout the country. The Communists invalidated the old kroner of the overthrown government. People literally threw money at each other in the streets. Overnight we became poor. Paupers."

Jason paused in his narrative. His eyes glowed with the memory of distant pleasures. He filled two more glasses. We drank up, and he resumed his tale.

"Then one day I traveled to Budapest, hoping to trade a diamond brooch for gold or for dollars. The streets were crowded and noisy. Everyone had something red in their lapels. There was a relaxed atmosphere. Loud, bold talk. People singing. In the marketplace and in mid-street, gatherings—meetings. A man making a speech from the top of a tram. When he was done, the crowd sang.

"As I was crossing a street . . . you'll never guess what I ran into. I saw a group of Hungarian soldiers, fully armed, carrying high a red flag on which was written in Yiddish, 'International Red Regiment,

Jewish Contingent.' I was excited—delighted to see the Jewish letters and Jewish faces. I looked closely at the soldiers and recognized two of them from my hometown: Zainvel, Hersh Schuster's son; and Maier, the son of the sexton.

"I cried out, 'Zainvel, Maier!'

"They recognized me. 'You're here too?' they cried, flinging themselves on me, embracing me. They explained that the Austrians had sent them to Hungary in work gangs. 'We're going to conquer the world. The power of the workers will triumph,' they added. 'We can't talk to you now. We're on patrol. Come tonight to the Café Lenin on Tefi Street. We'll talk more there.'

"On that same day, the war between Romania and the Hungarian Red Army broke out. Volunteers signed up for service on every street corner, and weapons were handed out. That evening I saw the two young fellows from my hometown. They persuaded me to enlist in the Red Army. I was sorry for Ella, but the passionate crowds and the excitement had turned me into a loyal soldier of the revolution. I sent Ella a note and the fifty dollars I had gotten for her brooch. 'Take care of yourself, Ella. It may be a while before we see each other again.'

"I spent two weeks learning to handle a rifle. Then, because of my strength, I was made a section leader and sent to join the battle against the Romanians."

Jason poured two more glasses, took a deep drag on his cigarette, clinked his glass with mine, and drank his spirits down at a gulp. It was now very warm in the tavern. As I looked about, I was aware that the young waiter was standing some distance away, staring at Jason as if he were a visitor from some other world.

Seeing that he had been observed, the waiter came slowly toward us. Shyly he said to Jason, "I know who you are."

"Ah, so you know me." A fleeting, pleased smile appeared on Jason's face, which was now ruddy because of the alcohol he had drunk, the excitement of his narrative, and the warmth of his own vigorous body. "You know me? Well then, tell me, who am I?"

"You're Jason, the champion."

Jason smiled.

"I saw you in a match at the Vangoli Circus. You're the best of the champions. You've got the others all beat. Jason . . . I'll see you at the circus on Sunday." With that he ran off into the depths of the bar. Even at a distance we could hear the lad's voice: "Do you know who we've got with us?"

"Who, Antek?" several drunken voices cried.

"Jason. The champion, Jason."

"What's the dear fellow doing here?" The voice that reached us was rasping, drunken. I could tell it belonged to the droshky driver.

"He's drinking schnapps."

". . . have to go see him."

"Yes, we've got to pay our respects," several fellows chimed in.

We heard the stumbling of unsteady feet, the sound of glass-laden tables groaning like tortured creatures as they were run into by bodies that could not maintain their balance.

Several people, flushed and sweating and moving with great difficulty, came up to us. Their bleary eyes misted over and their hair was wet. The hair under their unbuttoned coats and jackets was moist. Their hands were wet and sticky from slobber and other moisture that the alcohol produced in their bodies. They looked as if they had slept in a mire all in a heap and had warmed the muck in which they had just now awakened and had come to us in the bar. There were two women in the crowd, also drunk. One had a mouse's thin lips and balding patches of hair of an uncertain color—neither dark nor blond. Her blouse was torn, and one could see her pale soft body glistening with sweat. Her skin showed the clear marks of bites from some man's large teeth. The teeth in her own mouth were black and like those of a horse. She laughed continually, a foolish drunken laughter that sounded like a wheeze. The other woman was short and stout. The defeated look on her wrinkled face was enlivened by the fires of alcohol. Her eyes had such deep blue circles under them that she looked as if she was wearing spectacles from which the lenses had been lost. Her mouth was wide—exceptionally wide—and her wary laughter made it seem wider. Each of these women had her waist encircled by some man's arm.

The droshky driver stepped out of a dense cluster of people and bowed. "Greetings to our champion, Jason."

Jason rose and bowed to them all. The two musicians stopped playing. They stood on tiptoe trying to see over the crowd that stood behind the droshky driver, trying to get a glimpse of Jason.

"Long live Jason, our champion," one of the women called.

"Here's to Jason. Here's to Jason," the crowd repeated.

The other woman snatched a bottle of spirits out of some ragged fellow's hand and pushed her way through the crowd to Jason and filled his glass. With the bottle at her lips, her voice inflamed, she cried hoarsely, "I drink to your vigor, Jason."

Jason drank.

The racket increased. The old man beside the buffet suddenly became mobile. He moved forward toward the crowd that surrounded us.

"Hey musicians, play a march in honor of the world-renowned master, Jason," the droshky driver yelled. Then, over the heads of the crowd, he threw several coins to the two musicians standing beside the pillar in the middle of the room.

The musicians moved into action quickly and started to play.

The two women seized Jason, formed a circle, and danced with him. The whole crowd danced along on unsteady feet, making a wild, drunken circle and shouting incomprehensible cries.

Jason danced with them all.

The tavern owner lowered the shutters. It was already midnight, and it was no longer legal for the place to be open. He ordered the musicians to stop playing so their music wouldn't be heard in the street, betraying the presence of the crowd inside. As for the people themselves, he urged them to move deeper into the bar, to make it harder for the yelling and the racket to reach the street.

At about one o'clock Jason and I left the Carlos Bar. Jason was half drunk. He held my arm, and both of us walked with uncertain steps along the street.

At the corner of a busy street Jason shouted, "Droshky." A droshky drew up and we got in. "Hotel Klukass."

The cold air was refreshing. We breathed deeply, ridding ourselves of the polluted air of the bar. For more than a quarter of an hour we rode in silence. Jason was the first to speak. "Where do you live?"

I made no reply.

"Why don't you answer?"

"I don't live anywhere."

"What does that mean?"

"I've only recently been discharged from the Polish army. I haven't succeeded yet in renting a place. I've slept in the circus for the last several nights."

"Tonight you'll stay with me at the hotel. I'll rent a double room with two beds. Oh yes, I've met intelligent, decent people in my time who haven't had a place to sleep."

My mention of the army reminded Jason about himself. "Oh yes, I haven't yet told you what happened to me after I went off to the front with the Hungarian Red Army. Listen." And he resumed his narrative.

"After we beat the Czechs, we were sent to the Hungarian-Romanian border. The Romanians had massed a huge army made up of their own soldiers and Hungarian White Guard deserters who served side by side with the Romanians. The White Guards shot every Red soldier who was captured—but only after torturing him atrociously. In battle after battle we beat the Romanians, driving them far back behind the Hungarian border. We celebrated our victory with wine, music, and dancing. The wine flowed like water, but the Romanians weren't asleep. They were very sneaky young fellows. The main body of their troops, together with the White Guards who were ostensibly sent to engage us in decisive combat, did not meet us in battle. Only a few of their regiments fought us, and it was those we had beaten.

"But beyond that, we were the victims of an ugly betrayal. A Slovak general who claimed to be the son of a smith—thereby gaining Bela Kuhn's trust—was, at the behest of the people's government in Budapest, given command of a division of the revolution's most loyal, most enthusiastic volunteers—the pride of the Communist regime. It was this "steel" division that had, like a threshing machine, cleared the Hungarian fields of foreign enemy; and it was on this division that everyone's hopes were pinned. It was meant to be the bastion—the steel armor of the Communist state.

"The Slovak general, who had sold himself to the Romanian general staff and to the aristocratic Horthy, led this division into a mire and permitted it to be encircled by the main Romanian army and White Guardists. For two weeks in a row the troops of the steel division fought, starved, used up their ammunition, and quarreled with each other in despair. For a week they fought the enemy using guns without ammunition, daggers, swords, knives. My friend, since you've been to the front, you'll know what it means to fight for so long with cold guns.

"The result was that almost everyone in the steel division was either destroyed in battle or was slaughtered after being taken prisoner. The remnants of the international regiment did not retreat. They fought on. One soldier after another fell. The sexton's son, Moshe, died in my arms. With a bullet through his chest, he breathed his last without making the least small cry. There were eighty of us who survived. With no other recourse, we decided to head back to Hungary.

"In a Hungarian village we were captured by the White Guard. We knew what our fate would be: our faces to the wall, a bullet in our backs. We waited calmly to die. Death, however, did not come so quietly. The White Guards amused themselves with us, ridiculed us, tormented us. They put ground bricks into our food. They put ashes and urine in our wine. They drove us into the village marketplace, where they forced us to dance. They tied cats to our shoulders, then took pot shots at the cats. Sometimes they hit the cats; sometimes they hit us and not the cats.

"One time when they were driving us about the market square I saw a woman in the crowd whose face looked familiar. She was walking along conversing with an elderly White Guard officer. I tried my best to get a good look at the woman.

"'Ella,' I cried in a voice that seemed not to be my own. Yes, it was indeed Ella, the wife of the Romanian prison director. The woman with whom I'd run away. 'Ella!' I called again. This time she heard me, and recognized me. I could see that she turned pale, that her slim body trembled. But she kept silent and made no gesture of acknowledgment.

"The next morning we were led to the marketplace again. Our hands were tied, and we were forced to undress and to lie down half naked on the ground. Our shoulders were smeared with ground meat mixed with human excrement and animal dung. Each man lay half a meter or so away from the other. Then more than a hundred pigs were driven into our midst. The pigs, squealing wildly, tore at our naked shoulders. Not far from us, thousands of people looked on, delighted by the atrocious spectacle. Many of the prisoners had parts of their shoulders gnawed away by the pigs.

"Then the pigs were driven off, our hands were untied, and we were ordered to get to our feet. It was then that I saw Ella again. She was so pale she seemed about to faint, hardly able to stand on her feet. There were tears in her large beautiful eyes. As I was marched past her, I heard her calling faintly, tenderly to me: 'Sivo.' It was my Slovakian name. 'Sivo.' The tears in her wide eyes grew larger, brighter.

"Two days later we were brought to trial. It was hardly what one would call a trial. Two generals and a regimental commander identified seventy of us as Communists—members of the Party, and volunteers. Over and above that, our regiment was charged with the murder of ten White Guard officers. We were condemned to be shot by a firing squad. The punishment was to be carried out the next morning.

"I lay on my plank bed and waited to die. I thought of everything and about nothing. I had not the slightest hope of a rescue.

"'Too bad. I'm going to die.'

"It was raining when they marched us out into the field to carry out our punishment. We marched, downcast, hunched over, ready to die. A young French sailor marched near me. He had his hands in his pockets and tried to encourage me by whispering, 'We'll get even with them in the next world.' It was a joke at which nobody laughed.

"We were brought to a halt in an empty field that was hidden on one side by a row of hills and by a forest on the other. Once again the verdict of the court-martial was read to us. Just as the officer had finished reading and the order was given to bind our eyes, a rider waving a document galloped up furiously. He came to a stop not far from us. Dismounting from his horse, he approached the commanding officer and handed him the document.

"Some moments passed while the officer read it. Then he told his men to stop tying our eyes. His troops obeyed.

"'Sivo Kirbit,' he cried, turning to the condemned prisoners.

"I remembered that that was my name. My assumed name. 'Here, sir,' I replied.

"'Untie that man,' the officer said, turning to his troops. The ropes around my hands were untied.

"'Sivo Kirbit. You are a free man. You may go wherever you like,' the officer told me.

"My soul was flooded with joy. Was it possible? Was I really free? Was I really meant to live? I could not believe my eyes. The whole sequence of events felt like a strange, obscure dream.

"'Sivo Kirbit, step out of the ranks.' Again the officer turned toward me.

"I stood paralyzed for another couple of minutes, not knowing what was happening to me. Finally I understood that I was supposed to leave my unfortunate comrades. I moved quietly away. Those of my comrades whose eyes were as yet unbound—some twenty or twenty-five of them—watched me, their eyes wide, uncomprehending. Eyes in which there gleamed envy and hatred, as if they were looking at a traitor. But how could I explain to them that it was not my fault that my destiny was not the same as theirs?

"I left the dreadful place.

"Ella. It was Ella who had saved me. She loved me. She loved me with all the fiery passion of her Magyar blood. I was overwhelmed with gratitude and with grief that I had left her without saying goodbye, without having held her in my arms.

"A peasant from whom I inquired pointed out the way to Budapest for me. I hadn't gone far when I saw a coach coming toward me. Even at a distance I could tell there was a woman in it. She cried out and raised her hands in a gesture of joyful surprise.

"'Ella,' I called. I stopped in the field where I was. I could feel my whole body trembling."

The droshky in which Jason and I were riding came to a stop before the Hotel Klukass, an inexpensive hotel in Lodz. We got out.

Jason had his room changed for one with two beds. He sat back in a chair and resumed his narrative.

"The story of Ella isn't finished yet. We were to endure and experience a great deal more. After she rescued me we went off to Budapest.

"Ella explained that I owed my freedom to her father, a high-ranking Hungarian officer. At first he had refused to do anything to help me. Though Ella wept and pleaded with him for four days in a row, he continued to refuse. Then, on the fifth day, she tried to hang herself. It was only then that her frightened father managed to arrange for my freedom.

"Ella and I ran off together, leaving her father's home. We had very little money. We went to Austria, where we spent several months. Our money began to dwindle away and we had to think seriously about earning a living. I looked for a job in Austria but could find nothing. I wasn't used to heavy labor—I'd never done that sort of work before. We went on to Czechoslovakia. Ella was a talented dancer and a skillful horsewoman. As for myself, you can tell from looking at me that I was not what you'd call a weakling. And so we both joined a wandering Czech circus called the Kludki. At first they weren't willing to take us unless we could produce circus performers' papers, but Ella persuaded the circus director to let her demonstrate her skill as a dancer and a trick rider. He agreed to let her try, and he loved her performance. We were allowed to join the circus—at low pay."

Jason paused in his narrative. There was a glint of tears in his eyes. He turned his head away and looked off into the distance as if he were seeing in the air an unwinding panorama of his experiences. The lips of this massive man were pressed tightly together as if sealed by his newly recalled grief.

"Our circus traveled to Poland. We made guest appearances in Galicia. By that time Ella and I had become performers of the first rank in the circus. We were playing the town of Zlotchev, below Lemberg. It was a warm summer evening. After she had done her number, Ella went outside not far from the circus for a breath of fresh air. As she stood there, trying to refresh herself in the cool evening breeze, a man leaped out at her and shouted, 'You don't recognize me, do you?'

"Before Ella could reply, the man threw her to the ground and cut both her breasts off with a huge sharp knife.

"Her dying cry was heard inside the circus. The word 'murder' swept through the audience, and I was among those who went outside. God help me—there was Ella expiring in the street in her own blood. She died in my arms. Died kissing me. Whispering with her last strength, 'Forgive him . . .'

"The murderer was arrested. I tore my way through the police and through the people who had grabbed him when he tried to escape. I got my hands around his throat and squeezed. When he was finally torn from my grasp he showed hardly any signs of life.

"The murderer was the Romanian, her husband. In the course of his trial in a Polish court a letter was received from the Romanian consul, who had been asked for information about him. The letter informed the court that he had been a prison director in Romania. That the police had arrested him there on a charge of embezzling state funds, as well as for certain sexual crimes committed on women who had been arrested and sent to his prison. After his arrest he had fled to Poland. And there in the traveling Kludki Circus he had found

Ella. The Polish court sentenced him to twelve years in prison. At the end of twelve years he would be sent to Romania, where a Romanian court would try him for his theft of state money and for the crimes he had committed in the prison he had once directed."

Jason's story was done. He sat quietly in his chair, his eyes lowered. I sat opposite him, looking into his broad, grief-shadowed face. We sat without speaking for several minutes. Then the silence was broken when a hotel waiter came in. He asked, "Will Herr Jason have something to eat?"

"No, I've already eaten," Jason replied like one who has just wakened from sleep. He turned to me. "But you'll have something, won't you?"

"No. No. I've also eaten," I replied. The waiter left the room. A few minutes later each of us went to bed.

18

The next evening at five I showed up at the Venus Cinema. The manager was not yet there. I asked the young woman who was sitting in the ticket booth when he was due. She said he was expected at any minute. Meanwhile I waited around out in the street.

Though it was the middle of the week, large numbers of workers were beginning to fill up the small auditorium of the movie house. The weavers were on strike, so they had plenty of time on their hands. And with money in their pockets from their recent weeks' wages they could afford to come to the movie. They came with their wives. Some wore their Sunday cloth suits; some wore colorful dresses. Others wore their workaday patched clothes with dark oil spots left by the weaving machines.

On their way to the movie house, in the doorway, and in the lobby they discussed the latest meeting with the bosses. One worker who had just come from a union meeting in town reported that the Minister of Labor had come to Lodz to persuade the workers to accept the five percent raise the manufacturers had offered and to return to work. A crowd of weavers gathered around this man while he was giving his excited report. The crowd cursed the manufacturers, repeating frequently, "We'll keep striking. We want all our demands met."

Then another worker showed up, bringing news from the union that the textile workers in Girardov and Bialystok had decided at their meetings to strike as a way of strengthening the Lodz strike still further. A couple of minutes later another messenger arrived. He was breathless but joyful as he cried, "Comrades. General strike!"

The crowd hummed around him like flies. They surrounded him and, tugging at his jacket, demanded more and more details. He could hardly catch his breath; his chest heaved. His speech was fragmented, and, as he talked, he waved his muscular brown arms that were stained with factory vapors, soot, and machine oil.

"The minister came . . . automobile from Warsaw . . . also in the Grand Hotel. Summoned delegates from Socialist textile union and from the National Workers Union. Communists yelled . . . not to go to any conference with a minister, but to keep striking until all demands were met. Socialists urged going. A fight. The seventy-year-old Communist Rikhlinski got up . . . banged on the table . . . said, 'Softly, children. We ought to hear what their minister has to say. Listen—then do what we want.'

"'Bravo!' the Socialists shouted. Wanted to carry the old Communist on their shoulders. The Communists quieted down . . . quit their racket.

"A delegation was elected and sent to the minister. Grandpa Rikhlinski was elected to the delegation . . . unanimously . . . by the Socialists and the Communists. They all voted for him. When Grandpa heard that he was included in the delegation, he laughed. 'Don't send me to any minister. I'm afraid I'll tell him off—him and his father.' They went to the minister without Rikhlinski. But nothing came of the meeting. The minister argued that the manufacturers could not offer any more. That the workers would accomplish nothing with their strike. Just the opposite. They would lose time and work. The delegation left him with nothing.

"After the meeting with the minister there was a conference of all the unions. The decision: general strike. There'll be no tram running in town tomorrow morning. There'll be no gas or electricity. All the workers will be on strike."

"Hurrah for the general strike!" The cry went up on all sides. "Hurrah for the strike! Hurrah! Hurrah!"

I stood by, listening to the weavers' heated shouts. Then the manager of the Venus Cinema came in. Seeing the crowd gathered in the lobby, he smiled contentedly. I came up to him. He recognized me.

"Yes! You'll be on stage right away. Just wait a minute. I want to step into the ticket booth." He returned almost at once. I followed him backstage.

"See, you'll be standing behind the screen, the way you are now. So you can't be seen. And you'll speak in a loud voice, so that you can be heard all the way into the street. But you won't say anything at the first showing. You just watch the film so you'll know what's going on."

He disappeared. I was left standing there.

The projectionist in his booth gave some sort of a signal to indicate that the first show was about to begin. The auditorium filled with workers—men and women. There was a hubbub of voices, as at a stormy meeting. Everyone was talking about the general strike.

Two Orphans, a film by Moretti about the great French Revolution, was being shown. The audience, feverishly excited by the strike, watched impatiently, restlessly, their heads in constant motion. The air smelled of meetings, demonstrations, protests, machine oil, and the bodies of the workers.

The first showing was over. The auditorium emptied out, only to be filled to capacity with a new crowd of dejected textile workers. Before the second show began, the manager mounted the stage and, bowing on all sides, his face overflowing with loving smiles, made a "short" speech.

"Ladies and gentlemen," he began. "For the pleasure of my distinguished patrons, for your entertainment pleasure I have invited a narrator who will describe the films for you. I have spared neither trouble nor expense to bring this famous narrator to Lodz and to the Venus Cinema. In order to buy his contract from the theater where he formerly worked I had to pay a fantastic sum of money. The narrator whose voice you will shortly hear has enchanted audiences that numbered in the hundreds of thousands. The Fascists wanted him to work for them, and said they were prepared to pay him five thousand dollars a month. The Comintern in Moscow offered him ten thousand dollars. Yes, ladies and gentlemen, ten thousand dollars a month.

"He must be rich if he turned it down," said a voice.

The manager was caught up in the excitement of his speech. The words "Communists," "Fascists," "thousand dollars" spurred him to talk still more.

I laughed. I fully expected that after the manager had done speaking about me I would be hooted off the stage. I thought, "Thank God the audience won't be able to see my face as I talk."

The manager plunged on: "I have personally seen a letter of his in which Trotsky invited him to address millions of people over the radio. But the narrator is not a party person, and from his point of view Trotsky is no different from Mussolini."

It suddenly struck him that he was advertising me wrong. He adjusted his spectacles and changed his tone. "Ladies and gentlemen, he is one of you. He is a worker, like yourselves. Flesh of your flesh, blood of your blood. Not long ago he was so poor he hungered for a bit of bread. He walked about ragged, barefooted. Then he achieved his brilliant career."

The manager's speech was boring the audience. Several of the workers laughed in his face.

"That's enough," someone shouted, the words hard as a fist.

"Enough chitchat. Let's hear the narrator."

It finally reached the manager that he ought to quit talking. He smiled, bowed several times, and left the stage, saying, "And now, workers, the show begins. You are about to hear the famous narrator."

My impulse was to run. After all, what sort of a speaker was I? Where did I get off giving speeches? I'd never spoken to a large audience. The manager had set me up.

"Well," said the manager, clapping me on the shoulder as he left the stage, "now we'll see what you can do."

I made no reply. I waited, prepared to be hooted off the stage. There was a final signal, and the house grew dark. A bright stream of light spurted from an opening in the projectionist's cubicle. Shapes began to move on the screen.

Fearing disaster, I started to speak.

". . . and the great masses of the French people could no longer endure the yoke of the despotic King Louis the Sixteenth, and, one sunny day, they took to the streets of Paris, roused by a desire for freedom and justice inspired in them by the words of the prophets of the revolution, Danton and Saint-Just. Their hearts filled with song and a love of life, their powerful arms raised, they stormed and overthrew that bastion of oppression, the Bastille.

"'Danton, spirit of the revolution,' the masses cried, turning to their prophet, 'lead us to victory. Take our bodies and our souls, and rid France of despots and of tyrants. Bring light to our dark cellars and hovels. Rid the land of swindlers and thieves. Keep our children from death, and our wives from coughing themselves to death with tuberculosis. Cleanse the leeches from our bodies; the leeches that suck our blood. Our blood poisoned by microbes in our filthy workshops and factories. Danton, spirit of freedom, make a steel armor of our hearts and breasts, an armor that will contemptuously turn aside the bullets of Louis's vassals, and those of his low underlings.'"

I spoke loudly, with heat and passion. I could hear the silence descend on the crowd as it drank in my words. "And Louis the Sixteenth's artillery and machine guns opened their metal mouths and began to spit fire and lava at the revolutionary people. The revolutionaries, their breasts bared, and armed only with axes and scythes, began a struggle against the Swiss Guards, the hired soldiers of the despot—a struggle against cannon and machine guns.

"And the children of justice and freedom triumphed. They toppled the Bastille. Captured Louis. Drove off the Swiss. Destroyed the throne. The flag of freedom fluttered on high. The sounds of 'The Marseillaise' echoed the message, 'People of France, free yourselves.'"

When the first reel was done and the lights went on, the audience burst into stormy applause. "Hurrah for the narrator!" My speaking had pleased the workers—especially now, with the coincidence of the general strike. The auditorium was noisy. Everyone spoke of the film, about me, and about the French Revolution. Everyone talked, quarreled, shook their heads, waved their arms, or moved about. Everyone in the auditorium participated in the tumult. Everyone—men, women, and children. When the film showed the masses dancing in the streets, several pale, sad-eyed women whose faces reflected their poverty burst into tears. The audience got heavily to its feet and, mouths open, breathing hard, began to sing "The Marseillaise." Four times in a row the musicians were compelled to play "The Marseillaise" and after that "The Red Flag."

When the crowd began to sing, the manager ran in. His eyes wide, he cried desperately, "I'll get closed down for this." He turned and ran abruptly out, only to return again, pale with fear. "Stop singing Communist songs," he wailed. "They'll close the theater. I'll lose my livelihood."

No one paid the slightest attention.

When Danton appeared on the screen, the audience gave him an ovation. Their faces lighted up; they smiled delightedly at him; they waved their caps at him.

"Hurrah for Danton! Hurrah, hurrah, hurrah!" they shouted repeatedly. When Louis appeared, he was hooted. When the aristocrats were made to "cross the border," their deaths were greeted with ridicule and gallows humor.

"Rats!"

"Rats in aristocrats' clothing."

"Hey, on your feet! Get a move on!"

"Look out, Danton, they're getting away."

When Robespierre appeared, there was an incident. Because of his stern features and his rigid, forbidding manner, the audience took him for an aristocrat. When his image first appeared there were tumultuous cries of "Down, dummox" and "Off with you, evil spirit" directed at the screen.

Suddenly an elderly worker rose to his feet. Waving his arms angrily, he pushed his way through the crowd, climbed up onto the stage, and, standing beside the screen, turned furiously toward the audience. "Do you know who he is?" he pointed toward Robespierre.

"A dummox, that's who he is. One of Louis's partners."

"Not so loud, dummy." The older man stamped his foot. "That's Comrade Robespierre, *Robe ess pierre*. Now do you understand? Before ever Trotsky's father was born, Comrade Robespierre was already a Communist. Now do you understand?" he shouted contemptuously at the audience.

There was a moment's silence in the auditorium.

"How do you know?" someone asked the worker on the stage.

"How do I know? Because I know the history of the French Revolution. I've read some twenty books about it. I've got a book at home with Robespierre's portrait in it. I recognized him here at once."

"Hurrah for Comrade Robespierre," came an apologetic cry from someone in the audience.

Then, all at once, the film was interrupted. The lights went on. The audience waited for a few minutes. Then, when the film did not begin again, there began a stamping of hundreds of feet against the floor. Still the film did not come on again. A racket went up: shouts, yells, hoots. Several furious workers ran out into the corridor, where they found the projectionist sitting at the buffet, drinking a glass of beer.

"Why aren't you running the film?" they asked, their manner angry, threatening.

"The machine's broken down."

"Don't give us that. Tell the truth. Why aren't you running the film?"

The projectionist said nothing for a moment or two and continued to drink his beer.

One of the workers slapped him on the shoulder and said, "You're being asked a question. Do you hear? Why isn't the film running?"

"Why? Because I've been ordered not to."

"We'll show you who gives orders around here. The manager or us. We pay for the tickets. We give the orders. Not the manager." They grabbed the projectionist by the arms and shoulders and dragged him into the projection booth.

"Get a move on, brother. Start up your barrel organ," they said, pointing to the projection machine. Meanwhile the audience continued its racket, stamping on the floor. One of the workers peered through the hole in the cubicle through which the film was projected and shouted to the audience, "Quiet down. He's going to start the film."

The projectionist restarted the film. The workers locked his door, took the key away with them, and went back into the auditorium. There the film was running; the lights went out.

Out in the corridor a depressed and desperate manager ran about. He did not want to call the police. What worried him was that if the police arrested any of the workers, his theater would be boycotted and he would lose his income.

In the auditorium the hubbub continued. Whenever there was a scene that especially pleased the audience, a shout went up: "Hey, projectionist, reverse your barrel organ. Show us the guillotine again." The projectionist put his head into his peephole and complained with tears in his eyes that it was hard to do, but no one in the audience believed him, so he had to do what they ordered.

19

The next day I ran into Jason on the street. He was strolling quietly through the city center. He shook my hand warmly and chided me for not having come to stay with him at his hotel. It was nearly eleven o'clock in the morning. There were no tramways running.

The town had a sleepy, weary look. Reinforced police patrols moved through the streets. They were getting ready to deal with demonstrations by the weavers. The shops were closed; their bored employees stood around in the doorways yawning up at an overcast sky. The air still had in it the smell of a lingering autumn that stubbornly refused to give ground to the oncoming winter. Yesterday's light frost had entirely disappeared. Not a trace of it anywhere. In the frost-swollen cracks between the paving stones there were slim rivulets of mud glistening like bits of shattered mirror reflecting the overcast, windblown sky and the overhead trolley wires which, now, looked like the suspended arteries of some gigantic beast.

"Where did you sleep last night?" Jason inquired.

"In the home of a worker. A Gentile." I told him of my new profession and all that had happened yesterday in the Venus Cinema. In his beautiful light brown eyes there was a gentle, kindly glow, a gleam of rare geniality. He listened attentively to all I had to say.

When I finished, he smiled and said, "That's a strange story. So you were a triumphant speaker? It's an unusual profession, though not exactly a new one." Then he added, "In Romania, where illiteracy is widespread, there's always someone in the movie houses who explains what's happening on the screen."

I said, "I guess I was a success. After the film was over there was a great crowd of people who came up on the stage, curious to see me.

Several of them shook my hand and said I was a good speaker. It's all very funny. I've never in my life spoken before an audience, and here I am being complimented on how well I speak. When I suggested that I needed a place to spend the night, several hands went up. They literally fought to get me. I spent the night in the home of a respectable Gentile family. They gave me a bed all to myself. I was treated with the greatest respect, and they wouldn't let me go until I had eaten breakfast."

"Tonight," Jason said, "I want you to come and stay with me. Is that clear?"

"Perhaps I will."

"You have to promise."

"Yes."

Just then a wealthy, elegantly dressed woman went by. Her wide eyes looked hungrily into Jason's, and she gave a fleeting smile—as if he was someone she knew. Jason returned her look and smiled back, but he did not greet her. A few moments later the woman returned and fluttered her handkerchief at Jason. He turned his head and took no notice. The woman looked after him, an avid look on her face.

"Do you know who that woman is?" Jason asked me.

"No, I don't."

"She's the daughter of a well-known local manufacturer. Let me tell you how I know her.

"After our first performance in Lodz, I received a note containing a full-scale declaration of love. The note informed me that I could meet the writer in the Grand Hotel. The room number was written down.

"After my work in the circus is done, there isn't much to do. One doesn't feel like going to sleep. And one is in a strange town. So, yielding to an impulse to drive boredom away with some adventure, I agreed to meet the woman at the hotel.

"I arrived at the hotel and went up to the designated room. She was already there, dressed in satins and silks, and everything about her—her hair, her arms, her face—was heavily made up. I could see that she trembled the moment she saw me. I knew what that meant, and I smiled inwardly. As I came in she removed the embroidered silk shawl from her shoulders. She stood before me, an endless array of glittering rings and bracelets on her hands, her arms, her throat. Even at a distance I was assailed by her powerful perfume. She came near and looked directly into my eyes and smiled an enticing, lascivious smile.

"'You're beautiful, Jason,' she said. 'You know that I'm in love with you. You're young and as powerful as an oak.' She continued to say nice things to me and moved so close to me that I could feel the touch of her body against my arms. I looked intently at her and recognized the lusting look in her face, the hunger and thirst to sin with any vigorous man. I saw her for what she was: the essential whore, who is an absolute slave to male vitality. The sort of loose woman who, overtaken by sin, is caught up in a storm of lust and has to give herself at every opportunity. In a train, in a hotel, in a field—wherever. The man interests her only according to the degree of his physical strength and the skill with which he moves—and whether he has regular features. Every professional athlete has such a 'lover' in every town to which he comes. Sometimes he has several at once. Such 'lovers' write no letters; and when you leave town, they forget you like last year's snow. It may be that sometimes when lust torments them throughout a sleepless night and their weary bodies toss and turn on their soft beds, they may see you. They imagine you making a graceful leap in the ring, or grabbing your opponent, or holding him in a lock. They see you conquering. Making movements that excite female lust. Or else they see you in the most hateful moments of sexual intercourse—and themselves lying spent and weak in the arms of sin like a twig snapped in the wind.

"Such women can be found in the hundreds. In every city where our matches take place, they run after one, the way bitches haunt the places where dog killers slaughter male dogs. The wrestlers join them and spend pleasant nights drinking and making love, and when they leave they leave with their wallets stuffed with cash. Because such women pay for their sins with gold. They steal the money from their rich parents and bring it to us. You can get anything you want from them. And indeed many of us have grown rich because of them. The black, Bamboula, has a fixed price: twenty dollars a night. But he's a cunning, clever fellow, that black. He never gives more than two nights a week to it. He guards his strength.

"She took my arm and led me to the table. She poured two glasses of wine and bade me drink. I drank. After all, one gets very depressed in a strange town. Looking at me, she blushed. Her eyes roved over my face, then fastened themselves on my body. Then, to excite me, she stripped above the waist even as she feverishly pressed my foot under the table with her own.

"I pitied the unhappy woman. Nothing more. There was such pain, such anguish in her face. A look such as painters give to fanatic women. Passion for such women is frightful, grievous. It torments their hearts and sears their veins like glowing iron. For them sin is at once heart and soul—and life itself.

"She seized me in her bare arms and began to crawl all over me to entangle me like a spider. But all I felt for her was pity—and revulsion."

Jason paused. His manner changed. "Do I strike you as a pious fellow, a holy man who has dealings only with virtuous women who are drawn to honorable love? I'd have to be a fool to claim any such thing. Perhaps one *can* find a woman or two who knows how to love. Perhaps there are three who have hearts that fit them for love. But when I feel like sinning, I go to a whorehouse and choose one of the street women who sell themselves because of their poverty. And not one of those women who even in their mother's wombs are already destined to be whores, to give themselves to many men.

"Her eyes half closed, she said passionately, 'I love you, Jason.' Then, biting her lips, she pressed herself against me, winding her half-naked body around me like a snake. She could see—and feel—my lack of enthusiasm, but that only made her more desperate. And the despair inflamed her lust. She knelt before me and begged, clasping my feet in her bare arms, pressing them against her glowing breasts.

"I was sorry I had come to the hotel. She was a human being, after all, and deserved to be pitied."

I looked more closely into Jason's face and saw in it a dreamy, tender expression that seemed out of keeping with his wrestler's muscular build.

"That scene in the hotel lasted nearly an hour. She lay whimpering at my knee. Then, casting aside all shame, she flung her clothes off and stood before me as naked as the day she was born. She began to dance, turning and leaping. Then she threw herself once more at my feet and wept bitterly.

"I was overwhelmed with pity for her, but I could not uproot my feeling of revulsion. She lay at my feet for a dozen minutes, then she got up and went over to the table. She took out a hundred-dollar bill which, with her eyes lowered for shame, she dropped into my hand.

"Do you think I was insulted because she tossed the money to me? No, you'd be wrong to think that. I actually felt more sympathetic toward her.

"Then there came into my mind the thought of little Doli, the clown. A tubercular who coughs his lungs out after each performance. He sends three-fourths of such money as he earns to his old mother and his deaf-mute sister in Prague. As for himself, he lives in poverty, worn out by the illness he has given up trying to heal.

"I went into the other room of the suite and rang for service. I told the bellman to get me an envelope. I put the hundred-dollar bill into the envelope and instructed the bellman to deliver it to Doli. Then I went back into the other room and took off my clothes and . . ."

Smiling, Jason tapped my shoulder. "I see her at the circus every day," he said, concluding his story. "She hangs around me, follows me everywhere. Several times a week she sends me notes."

The snow fell more thickly now. The town was covered with a dark veil.

"Where are you going after your engagement in Lodz?" I asked.

"We don't know where yet, but never mind. Our tour manager will know where to send us."

"How did you happen to choose wrestling as a profession?"

"Ha, ha, ha." When he laughed, Jason displayed his strong white teeth. "What else could I have been? A shoemaker? A tailor? Perhaps a bookkeeper? A wrestler—a professional wrestler—ah, what magic there is in the words. You're allowed to get drunk, to insult the other fellow, to treat him like dirt—and you get admired for your shape, your muscles, your chest measurements. How can a wrestler's life be bad? Today you're in Lemberg, tomorrow in Lodz, the day after in Budapest. Today you're a Jew, tomorrow a Czech. The week after, you're a Dutchman or a Latvian. Why settle down in one place? Why get married and spend your life leading your kids to Hebrew school? I can't imagine myself doing it. I know what's coming. I'll drag around like this for a few more years with the circus, traveling in vans, performing feats of strength, doing tricks. I'll get old and lose my vigor and my muscles. Ah, God knows what I'll do then. Well, brother"—Jason took my arm and moved closer to me—"anyone who has put in so much as two years in a circus will never be able to settle down. He'll always have the itch to wander from country to country, to move through the world like the wind.

"Sometimes I ask myself what will become of me when I no longer have the strength to pin the other fellow's shoulder to the mat. But I do my best not to think of it, and I drive such thoughts out of my mind."

We walked more quickly because of the snow, which was now falling thickly. It had grown dark, as if evening had somehow blundered into the noontime world. Passersby with opened umbrellas hurried past. Jason led me into a coffeehouse and ordered tea for us. We sat in silence for a little while and drank our tea. There were two other people in the café. One was a Jew, a man with a narrow, pale face who was gulping the news from the pages of his newspaper as he sipped his tea. There was also an elderly, gray-haired woman wearing a long black cloak. She kept looking out of the window, waiting for the snow to stop.

Jason would not let me go. He insisted on taking me to lunch. After lunch he remembered that he meant to visit his friend, the sick Doli. He invited me to go with him. I didn't refuse.

20

Doli had a room high up in the fourth-floor home of a poor family. The landlord opened the door wide and led us into the farthest room, where Doli lay under a sea of blankets. As we were passing through the first two rooms, we noticed that the family bedding had been stripped and was piled on Doli's bed. He lay under the covers, looking pale and wan—his round, completely bloodless face was immobile. His large eyes were a melancholy blue and made him look like a doll that a capricious woman had forgotten in bed when giving birth.

When we came in he was dozing. The sound of our steps woke him. He opened his large anguished eyes, then smiled weakly when he saw us.

Jason said, "Sleep, Doli. We didn't mean to disturb you." He turned as if to leave.

"Oh no. You're not disturbing me. I'm dozing because I sleep too much. You may not know it, but people who sleep too much are always sleepy." Doli sat up and beckoned us to come closer. We approached the bed; the landlord set chairs out for us.

"Well, how're things, Doli?"

"Mine is an atrocious illness. It toys with me. It humiliates me. For example, all the livelong day I cough my lungs out. I cough and cough as though through a leather sack. But every night at eight-thirty I feel perfectly well. I get dressed and go to the circus, where I do my act. Every single day it's the same. My illness allows me to tell jokes to an audience, to make them laugh or cry."

"You'll recover, Doli," Jason said.

Doli looked at him, and there was a look of bitter humor in his lively eyes—eyes so active they seemed to dart about like fish in a bowl.

"I lie here all day with the feeling that I haven't got a whole bone in my body. Everything seems broken; everything hurts. There's a wind whistling through my lungs. I spit my heart and lungs out in blood. My head aches, and I feel that I'm losing my mind, that I'm about to go to my final reward. In short, that I'm dying. That's the way things are until eight o'clock in the evening. Then, the moment the clock in the next room begins to strike eight, I feel better. I feel lighter, easier. So much so that at eight-thirty I'm fully dressed and on my way to the circus. That's how it is, dear friends. Every evening."

Doli turned to me. "It seems to me that you do something in the circus."

"Yes," I said.

Jason introduced me. "A friend of mine."

Doli gave me a warm but candid and penetrating look. "It's pure comic theater," Doli said with a bitterly mocking smile that twisted his thin, bloodless lips. "Every evening Death gives me permission to go to the circus. Lying here all day, cut off from everything, I have begun to think that Death doesn't want to shut my impudent and sassy mouth. He—Death, that is—must be one of my greatest fans. When evening comes he takes his paws off my chest and stops choking me. He runs off to the circus and waits for me to come and make him laugh. Ha, ha, ha. He is my friend—Death, my fan."

On Doli's pale, exhausted features a moist tinge of scarlet now appeared. He started to gasp, to cough. Then he spat something red into a towel. "Each day, when I am at the circus, I have the feeling that I'll see Death there, sitting in the gallery, gnashing his teeth and laughing his wormy laugh at me. My friends, I swear I saw him there last night. I was so frightened when I saw that skeleton face of his, I burst into tears right there in the auditorium. Yes, I wept."

On the window-sill by Doli's bedside there were a couple of books and several empty morphine vials.

Doli was seized by a coughing fit once more. He cried out, then flung his arm up in the helpless way of someone drowning who waves a final time before going down. Talking had brought on the coughing fit. And yet the more he coughed, the more Doli seemed compelled to speak.

The room in which he lay had been neglected for a long time. It was unpainted and was damp in every corner. Opposite Doli's window was a huge brick building with countless windows that so effectively obscured the sky that the sun's light never reached his room. The courtyard below was narrow and dark.

"Never mind, " Jason said in a clear loud voice. "You'll see, Doli, you'll get better."

"Yes, I never think otherwise myself," Doli said. Then he was seized by a coughing fit again. His head thrashed about on the pillow. "It's ten years that I've been dying this way. Death has toyed with me in several countries. I've come to think of him as my friend. To put it another way, what would I do in a strange town on an ugly autumn day like today if he hadn't confined me to my bed? Wander about the streets? Hang out somewhere in a restaurant? Better to lie here in bed and rest my bones. Take my word for it, Death is curing me." Doli began to laugh. Then he coughed so hard his whole body shook.

He went on. "You know, when all is said and done, I am a wrestler too. I wrestle with Death. Sometimes he gets me by the throat, sometimes I get him, but as luck would have it, he gets more chances to win. Ha, ha, ha.

"What I've written my mother is this: 'Dear Mother, Things are going well with me. Things couldn't be better. All day long I sleep like a sultan; I get to have all my meals in bed. In the evening I perform. And at night I get to sleep again. It's true, Mother dear, that I sleep a bit too much. But is there anyone who wouldn't prefer to be lazy if he didn't have to earn a living? Old people say, *Lucky the person who can (and is allowed to) sleep.'*" With that, Doli started to cough once more. We could see that our sitting at his bedside incited him to talk, so we got to our feet, made our farewells, and left the room.

I parted with Jason in the street. But before I left, I had to promise I would come spend the night with him at his hotel.

21

Once again I was alone. I found myself thinking about the various people I had met recently. Good Lord, what a feeling of loneliness that healthy-looking, muscular wrestler Jason gives off. And Doli the clown, and Vogelnest the poet—what winds of solitude blow from them.

I had nothing to do, so I wandered about in the streets. Then I went back to the park, where I hadn't been for a considerable while. There was no one there because it was raining. I was wet, soaked through. Then I remembered the woman with the blue spectacles, the woman who thought I was a mugger when I offered to carry her clothes basket for her. The scene in which the good woman changed her opinion of me and handed me her basket to carry stood out sharp and clear in my mind.

I thought about how deep and secret human love is. I shuddered to think that I might never know love's secrets. Love's caresses. What it is that makes the human heart fall in love with a passing stranger, a wanderer who may never again appear before one's eyes.

I asked myself a simple, direct question: How can one understand such a sudden love for a desolate, weary traveler? I remembered a couple of lines from a poem of Baudelaire:

Praised art Thou, O Lord, who sends compassion
Into the hearts of horses, keeping them
From stepping on fallen drunkards in the street.

I tramped about, going from street to street until I found myself before the house I had lived in—the old shoemaker's house. I thought I'd take a look and see how things were at the old man's.

I went down into the basement and opened the door to his apartment. Except for him, there was nobody else in the place. He lay on his straw pallet. There were bottles of medicine lying nearby. He opened his eyes and looked at me but did not recognize me. Without asking what I wanted, he closed his fever-reddened eyes, as if it made no difference to him who it was who had come in. I stood in the room for a few minutes and looked about. The walls were green and moist, and there was a leather mound of shoes that had been tossed into a pile where they lay acquiring mold, as if no one in a long, long time had touched them. Except for the old man, there was no one there. I left the cellar.

Again it was evening. I went back to the Venus Cinema.

Fearful of a repetition of last night's scene, the manager of the movie house had changed the bill. He was no longer showing *Two Orphans*. Instead there was a film that had Eddie Polo in the starring role. During the first show I did no talking. Instead I watched the film and studied it for its content, so that later I would know what to say. The manager was not there. I went backstage, took a seat in a corner, and watched the action on the screen.

The movie house was in a low wooden structure—or, to put it better, it was in a sort of hastily built barracks. One could hear the slow, lazy sound of the rain falling on the roof. Mice ran about onstage. They took fright when they first saw me, and hid themselves in their holes, but later, as they got used to me, they grew bolder and crawled about openly on the floor quite close to where I stood. I felt dreary and cold. The panes in the small window high above the backstage area had been shattered, and the wind rushed in through the cracks. It shook the screen, then rushed off, only to return angrily again. At the beginning of the second show I started to speak.

I wanted to forget where I was, to intoxicate myself with lovely language, so I spoke of distant lands, of the rivers, seas, and mountains that rolled by on the screen.

"And the mountains are eternal, and their peaks are covered with snow, like the white hair of old age. And the sun loves to shine on the mountains, to give its golden rays as a gift to the rocks, as if it were warming children. And the sea, the great turbulent sea, loves to toss its silver waves at the foot of the mountains, the way a female slave might kiss and fondle her lord."

That was how I spoke, and I sensed a warmth in the words. Then I remembered the film's hero, Eddie Polo. I had entirely forgotten him.

"And now, the world-famous detective, Eddie Polo, appeared among these fabulous mountains on the hunt for the man who had burned down the millionaire Rosen's palace and who had murdered the vice-burgomaster's adopted daughter."

Then I spoke further about distant skies and new lands. I put my heart and soul into the words, and often I felt myself being transported by them to some distant place.

It was dark on the stage. Not a glimmer of light. The mice touched my feet, and one of them, a hungry one, tried to tear off a bit of shoe leather. A piercing wind enveloped me. I shivered with cold.

"And the ship, as if praying for stillness and rest, moved over the bosom of the turbulent and singing sea; and the waves leaped like tiny libertines around the ship. And the passengers traveling on business were hushed, and prayed in their hearts, 'Rock us, oh great sea; take us to a new land where light and freedom are eternal, and where there is sustenance for our wives and children, and where our souls may find joy and happiness.'"

Then, immediately: "And Eddie Polo went down into steerage

and searched among the ordinary, simple passengers. He had reason to believe that the murderer had disguised himself as a worker—an immigrant."

I spoke on, seeing no one. Nothing but the film. The sound of my words intoxicated me and made me forget everything else. The second showing of the film lasted a little more than two hours.

I sent the theater's errand boy out for food and had my supper onstage, washing it down with soda water from the buffet in the corridor. The intermission between the second and third showing of the film ended. I mounted to the stage again and started to speak.

In the dark the mice began to dance, to squeak for hunger. Once more they made an assault on my shoes but were repelled without success.

At eleven-thirty I was finished. Too much speaking had utterly exhausted me. My overstrained eyes hurt, and my head ached. I hurried away from the theater. I was so confused, so dazed, I saw nobody in the street.

From time to time I stopped to lean against a wall, to breathe more deeply. Then, hunched over, and with my collar pulled up, I went on. The rain wet me, and the wind whistled in my ears.

I didn't keep my word: I didn't go to Jason's hotel. Feeling emptied, ill, and not inclined to talk, I wanted to avoid conversation. I went instead to the family in whose home I had spent last night. The gate of the house in which they lived was shut, which reminded me that I did not live there, and that I had no right to disturb anyone's sleep at this time of night.

I made my way back to town and wandered about through the silent, dark back streets for another hour or so. I was unwilling to walk down the main streets because the light of the electric lamps hurt my eyes.

I still had a little money, so I went back to the home of the Jew who lived near the railroad station. I paid him and spent the night there.

22

The next day I arrived at work at the theater feeling quite ill. My eyes hurt; they were inflamed and red. But I was able to rest them because I remembered the plot of yesterday's film, and so I could keep them closed, though every so often I would peek at the screen just to make sure I wasn't making a mistake.

And that was how, with weary eyes, I stood recounting the heroic deeds of Eddie Polo. When I went out into the corridor at the end of the first show I ran into the manager.

"You're an exceptional narrator," he said. "The audience loves you."

"Perhaps you can let me have some money."

"Yes, of course." He took his wallet out of his pocket and handed me a bank note.

The last show was over. Shivering with cold, I left the stage and started off to the home of the Jew who lived near the railroad station. I meant to sleep there.

As I came out of the stage entrance, I saw that I was being watched intently by a pale, bright-eyed young woman with a smile on her lips. I glanced briefly at her but could not imagine why she would be interested in me. I went on, but in the street I noticed that the young woman was coming toward me, the same smile still on her lips. I looked more carefully at her. She was pale, very pale. Her extraordinary large eyes were radiant. Her thick blond hair framed her round face; her lips were thin and mobile. She wore a reddish cap and a gray coat. I could not understand the meaning of her glance. The smile on her red lips had in it a mixture of grief and compassion. I tried to absorb her face into my being. The closer she came, the more meaningful and warm her smile appeared to be. It seemed to shed a glow over her cheeks and lips. She passed by me, whispering, "Beloved," and went quickly away. By the time I turned to look after her she was already gone. Vanished.

"Beloved." The word rang in my ears. What did it mean? "Beloved." Was it the wind that whispered it? No. I must have imagined that someone had spoken to me that way. Who was the young woman who had looked at me so intently? What was the meaning of her smile? Perhaps it was all a mistake. Perhaps it was my loneliness, my sense of isolation from the world that was deceiving me, that compelled me to dream that a pale young woman was thinking of me. No, it was all a fantasy meant to relieve the dreary life of someone nobody thinks about. Maybe I was sick and seeing visions.

Her eyes had had a strange glow in them. What warmth, what goodness shone in them! And how much kindness there was in her smile! Her whole being was light and airy, like a vaporous, imaginary creature.

As I walked in the dark, I continued to see her large bright eyes.

For an hour or so I walked around this way. The stores were closed. I ate my supper at the railway station.

I found a place near the window and vaguely watched the comings and goings of people, of trains. The locomotives whistled and hissed. The dark heavy night made one think of the monotonous sound of boots tramping through muddy village streets into which a stubborn wind had flung a gloom stolen from eternally wandering clouds.

The strangeness of other unknown towns had settled on the dim, grimy windowpanes of the station and of the trains and seemed to be saying that their souls (the crowds of passengers) had been taken from them. A locomotive with several freight cars attached was quietly, carefully gliding away on the rails into the night-obscured far distance. The locomotive moved silently, without whistling, as if it was too ashamed to wake the bleak desolation that hung over the earth like a fog.

I followed the freight train's departure, my eyes fixed on the stream of tiny flames that sparkled up into the dark from the locomotive's smokestack.

And I was overwhelmed by a yearning to move on, move on, move on—anywhere at all.

I continued to look off into the distance, where the train was being swallowed up by the dark, where the flames grew smaller and smaller until they were completely extinguished.

The train station was almost entirely deserted. Two women with bundles and packages dozed against the wall. I returned to my lodgings to sleep.

The next day, during the intermission between the second and third show, a boy brought me a letter. On a piece of white paper were two words written in a fine hand: "Dearest one." Two words, and no more.

I searched the crowd in the lobby, hoping to see the pale young woman. My eyes wandered over the audience in the auditorium, but she was nowhere to be seen. Later, when, exhausted, I left the theater and was walking in the darkened streets, the young woman with the shining eyes came toward me. Trembling, I caught hold of her hand. She laughed a gentle, musical laugh, then tore herself from my grasp—and was gone. I stood transfixed for a long time, overwhelmed by surprise. Then I started to run, trying to find her. I ran feverishly through several streets, but the young woman was nowhere to be seen.

Who was this secretive, mysterious woman who was toying with me? What did she want of me? And what was the meaning of her letter? Why had she followed me? And why had she laughed at me? I thought and thought about her, and always I had her image in my mind—a pale young woman with large, compassionate eyes. I began to think that she might not be an earthly creature—that she might be from another world.

I imagined her veiled, with a halo around her head. And under her feet—neither earth nor floor of any kind. Only air—emptiness. She took possession of my mind like an unending dream that never leaves one, day or night.

Though I felt sleepy, I was convinced that I would come upon her in the streets that night, wandering about, her eyes glowing. So I searched for her everywhere until the gray light of dawn. I looked into the face of every passerby I met. All night long I searched for her, my mind continually fantasizing her. Sometimes I seemed to see her, her arms outstretched, ready to embrace me. Sometimes she seemed to stand as if in thought, aloof and proud, looking at me with her large eyes.

And, strange to say, that look in her eyes told me that she could see into every nook and cranny of my being, could see the loneliness that weighed like a mountain on my soul.

I looked for her every evening in the audience at the theater. Every night I hunted for her through the streets. But several days went by without a sign of her. She had disappeared.

She exhausted me; she tormented me. I searched for her every hour, every minute. There was no sign of her.

On the sixth day of my job in the movie house the errand boy brought me a letter.

"From her!" I cried joyfully, recognizing her handwriting. Feverishly I opened the envelope. A sheet of paper fell out.

I stood, stupefied. Several minutes passed before I came to my senses.

Darling,

I watched you sleeping in the street, in the rain. I stood at my window and watched you sleeping on the stone steps. I saw you, lonely and exhausted, lashed by wind and rain. I watched you wandering through the streets like a ghost as you carried the placard of the Circus Vangoli. I discerned your noble soul in your face, in your hands. I watched you, huddled in your soldier's greatcoat, moving about like a homeless dog through the park. I saw how you wished to give a girl your last bit of money because her childlike naiveté touched your heart. I followed you. For two nights in a row, dear wanderer, I could not sleep. I could not sleep because of you. My wealthy home became burdensome to me, and I went through the streets in search of you. I went to the manager of the circus to inquire where you might be, and through him I found you. The words that you speak in the theater when you narrate the film have revealed your anguished, weary heart to me. When I hear you speak, it seems to me that in your voice I hear the voices of all who are homeless, those who wander from city to city and who weep in the rain. Are you aware that you are *their* voice? Don't you know that you, only you are their soul? Aren't you aware that your blood is the autumn wind when the world is restless?

You are wondering, poor wanderer, why I write to you in this strange fashion. I know that you understand what I've been saying.

I have thought a great deal, a great deal about you. Perhaps as much as you have thought about me. I have wanted to see you, talk with you, go with you. My heart said, "Yes, go to him." But my judgment said, "No, don't go." I have followed my judgment.

I am very unhappy, dearest. Perhaps more unhappy than you are. I have a home, good parents, wealth, the best of everything. But I cannot find rest. My nights are ragged with sleeplessness, and my days pass wearily. I weep over every unhappy person, every hungry child, and for everything sad in the world.

I am sick, dear wanderer; my soul is sick. Before my eyes I see passing continually a series of black processions, long files of tormented people who have left our world, where they had neither homes nor rest. It may be that one day I will be in the forefront of such a procession, walking on and on over roads and highways with downcast head. I pray to heaven that after my death I may not find myself among those who are happy and fulfilled. Rather, I want to be among those who suffered.

Be well, darling. Perhaps we will see one another someday. It may be that I will come to you.

Those who hear you know that a soul weeps in your words.

Beloved . . .

There were tears in my eyes. The letter trembled in my hands.
The bell rang in the theater. The first show was about to begin.
Eddie Polo appeared.

23

I walked the streets for half the night thinking about the mysterious
woman. Exhausted though my mind was, I struggled to imagine her
again. And I succeeded. Her face was even paler, her eyes larger and
sadder than before. In the morning, when the street birds woke and
began their first song of the day, I returned to my lodgings at the home
of the Jew who lived near the train station. There I went to sleep. It was
late when I woke. Noon. I dressed quickly and went in to town.

The rain, which had been falling continually for the last several
days, now let up. It began to snow. The strands of white covered the
streets and the houses hesitantly, silently, as if they had arrived too
soon. I spent half an hour somewhere in a small restaurant, then I
walked the streets again.

I ran into Vogelnest. Even from a distance he recognized me. He
flung his arms out and greeted me warmly. "Why haven't you been
to see me?" he complained.

"I got a job recently, so I've been busy," I said, though inwardly I
wondered why I had let so much time pass without visiting him.

Vogelnest tossed his head impatiently, like someone who is
continually sleepless and confused. He talked constantly, in short
bursts of speech. And as if to himself, secretly.

"I'm thinking of leaving here . . . the town is beginning to feel ugly. A muddy, filthy town. And the people—cold and unfriendly. I'm sorry that I ever came here to begin with. What a town to have chosen," he cried bitterly, tossing his head even more frequently. "I've got an uncle here, a very rich man. Stuffed with money. Like a sack. So I went to him and asked him for a free loan with which to rent an apartment. So he says to me, 'Even when you were a child, people said you would come to no good.' Well, I got mad. Think of it—I come to a rich uncle, a man of fortune, a well-known yarn manufacturer, and I ask for a loan so I can get an apartment, so I can get out of the dank attic in which I live, and he digs up this old complaint. That when I was a child it was said of me that I would come to no good. Ha, ha, ha," he burst out, like a dog tearing itself loose from a chain. "I pointed out to him that he had no right to tell me anything about my childhood. That had nothing to do with him. He could either give me what I asked for or he could refuse. There was no need for him to be abusive. So he got angrier still and really began to abuse me. With the result that I ran out of there, slamming the door so hard the walls shook. He's a real pig. And lest you think he's been wealthy for a long time, let me tell you that he was a pauper until his thirtieth year. Went about begging money from his relatives. Many's the time he begged the price of a meal for himself, his wife, and his children from my father. Well, his luck changed. The wheel of fortune turned. He grew rich and learned to talk like a pig. I'm only sorry that I went to such a scoundrel for money."

Tossing his head constantly, Vogelnest cursed angrily, spewing bitter phrases like arrows. Then he caught himself up short, remembering something, and said, "Yes."

"Yes." And not another word. Then he ran off, but he kept looking back as if he wondered whether there was something he had forgotten to tell me.

24

That evening the movie house was closed. It was a holiday: *Bozhe Narodzenieh*, Christmas, when all performances were forbidden. I had free time. Once again I moved about the streets.

I returned to the street on which I had lived during the first few days after my release from the army. Wherever I saw light burning in a window, I looked in, hoping to see the room in which the pale young woman lived. I stared intently, trying to force my eyes to creep through the window curtains that hid the rooms from my sight. Who could tell where I might see her? There were many windows, and gas or electric light flickered in them all. It was a cold evening. In many places the sidewalks and the streets were covered with frost. Moreover, there was a piercing wind stalking about hungrily, licking at the earth, at buildings. A soft, hushed snow began to fall, making a delicate sound, as if silk threads were rubbing against each other. There were few people in the streets. A hurrying droshky flew by. The eyes of the horse sucked in the endless whiteness that shrouded the world on all sides. I walked about for a couple of hours, moving in a slow, leisurely fashion, examining every thing, every person, every droshky, every dog that I met. My habit of looking intently and boldly at them frightened several people, and they hurried away.

Once again I found my way to the train station. I stood at a window and watched a departing train. I loved the sound of the locomotive's whistle, the hiss of the boiler, the murmur of the wheels, and the sounds the workmen made signaling to each other. I spent half an hour this way, standing at the window of the train station looking out into the dark night as a train glided off on its steel rails and an incoming train arrived. My eyes accompanied all of the travelers—watched them settle into their seats, watched their turmoil, their hand motions, their hasty conversations with the people they were leaving behind. Only when the station was finally deserted, when there was neither an outbound nor an incoming train, when there was only a solitary locomotive on a siding, its engine cold, looking like a gigantic dead beast, an immobile steel corpse—only then did I begin to think of leaving.

A station workman, a pipe in his mouth, moved about over the poorly lit station tracks. Even from a distance the weary sound of his heavy, steel-shod boots could be heard. Each time he drew on his pipe the red glow in the bowl grew larger, as if its red brightness was competing with the gleaming little flame in the lamp near the station clock. On the other side of the tracks several scattered, isolated trees encrusted with snow swayed and bowed toward the dead locomotive, as if, together with the wind, they were singing a dirge that spread indignantly over the station tracks and took flight from there to the road that rolled endlessly toward the horizon, where the night with its teeth had entrenched itself in the earth and sky.

25

I woke up this afternoon at two o'clock. My landlord, a little yellow-bearded Jew with pale, withered features and quick, sly eyes which he closed at intervals as he talked—as if he were polishing the gleam in his eyes with his eyelids the way one polishes eyeglass lenses—my landlord said, "Forgive my asking, but what is it you do that makes you come home so late at night?"

I did not immediately reply. He became very apologetic. "Actually, it's none of my business. Properly speaking, I have no right to ask you. After all, what you do is not my business. Isn't that so? Not

my business. But, well, someone stays in my house . . . one is
curious."

"I don't do anything in the late hours. I just like to walk about at
night," I said.

"So!" he said, thinking the matter over as he gave me an intense,
gimlet-eyed look, as if he meant to trap me in some way, to learn
something. He shook his head sadly and went away. I could hear
him muttering for a considerable distance, "People now-
adays . . . entirely different . . . heads, heads . . . their heads aren't
right somehow."

I went out into the street and found my way to the house in which
the woman lived who had let me carry her basket of clothes. I went
up to her flat.

She was in her room, busy with a child whom she was bathing in a
large basin. The child's cries filled the room, and the mother was
trying to quiet it. The child stood in the basin like a puppy that has
been tossed into a stream to swim. Seeing me, the woman looked
about. She pushed back her eyeglasses with one hand and held the
child with the other.

"Good morning."

"Good morning. What do you want?"

"I owe you money."

Frightened, she stared at me over her glasses. "You owe me
money? Who are you?"

I took out several thousand-mark notes and put them on the table.
"You lent me money once."

"When? How?"

"Ah, evidently you don't remember at all. We met one night in the
street and you lent me money. That's the whole story."

She stayed there, kneeling on the floor like someone trying to
recall some long-forgotten event. "No, I don't remember. And if I
can't remember, I'm not going to accept any money from you. Take
your money back," she said excitedly, almost angrily.

I reminded her of the evening when I had offered to carry her
basket of laundry and she had mistaken me for a mugger; and how

later, when she realized her mistake, she had given me money. It was only when I had finished the tale that she struck her forehead, remembering the events of that night.

"So that was you. The soldier. Now I remember. Sit. Sit down." She got up from her kneeling position, leaving the child in the basin to leap about like a fish that has been thrown back into the water after its fins have been clipped. She pulled up a chair and set it down before me. "Sit, I beg you. Sit down. So you see. One doesn't get lost. If God wills it, one finds a job and lives like everyone else in the world. How are you? What are you doing? Where are you working? How are things?" she said, speaking quickly, throwing a hail of questions at me. I told her about my job. She listened openmouthed, and when I was done, she said, "Well, I can't say I'm happy about the job." She shook her head sadly, like a mother listening to a son's account of what he's doing. There was a warmth in her eyes as she looked at me. I felt like kissing her hands, and her dark gray hair.

I could see that I was keeping her from bathing the child, so I said goodbye to her, pressing her hand warmly.

"Do come back again, my dear. Drop in for a visit anytime. And don't worry. Things are sure to get better. But be careful, dear boy. Don't walk down any slippery paths."

Out in the street, I thought of the pale young woman again. It was dark, as if evening had stumbled into the afternoon. Muffled in shadows, I headed once again toward the street in which I had lodged when I first came to town. As I walked, my eyes anxiously searched the windows I passed. It was a quiet street. The windows were for the most part hung with curtains or drapes. There was not a face to be seen anywhere. Then, in a window on the second floor of a house with a facade of white plaster Roman pillars, the head of an old gray-haired man appeared. He stood stock still, engrossed in thought. He wore a grayish frock coat with silk lapels, and he looked like a tailor's mannequin displaying a new suit. I hung about for a while, sometimes on the left, sometimes on the right sidewalk of that quiet street, peering into every window of the houses there. Then I noticed that the old fellow in the frock coat was looking at me, scrutinizing my face and my pacing. I didn't feel like leaving but continued to look into every window. My heart beat more loudly in my breast.

Ah, how I longed to see the pale young woman, though truth to tell, I had no idea what I might say to her.

It got darker. The electric lights went on. The old man in the frock coat continued to watch me. He seemed to be frightened. His thin lips moved as he muttered something. His eyes followed me. I kept circling about in the street, looking into window after window. A light thin snow began to fall. I was covered with snow. The snow made the windowpanes gleam and glitter more brightly. The electric lights were covered with white. The snow made a caressing rustle as it fell. The deepening shadows gave a blue tinge to the white streets, the white houses. I kept on pacing, staring into windows, until I was rocked to sleepiness by emptiness and ardent yearning. I buried my head deeper into my collar and shoved my warm hands further into my pockets and went on stubbornly walking slowly back and forth on the sidewalk. The snow fell more thickly. I was wrapped in a thin white pelt of snow.

Sleepy and exhausted, I continued to walk the silent street, until suddenly I was startled to realize that I had forgotten to look into the windows. I opened my tired eyes, but my glance recoiled from the brightness of the electric lights. The snow encrusted on the lamps shimmered with a rainbow gleam. I cast a quick sleepy look up toward the windows and found myself trembling because I thought I had seen the pale young woman's eyes in one of them. I took up a position on the sidewalk in order to look at those eyes more carefully, more intently.

This time I did not see the eyes. I walked to the left and caught a glimpse of them again. When I stepped to the right, the eyes disappeared once more. "It's a kind of vision, a dazzle of light. An optical illusion deceiving me," I cried. I walked to the left of the house where I had seen the eyes. "Yes, I see them. Brown, large, beautiful, sad eyes. I see them." When I walked back a couple of paces, they disappeared. An elderly man went by, loudly tramping through the snow. Except for his nose, his face was entirely covered by his coat collar. I stopped him.

"Excuse me. Will you do me a favor?" I said, perplexed. "Do you see a pair of large eyes in that window?"

The man looked at me and muttered angrily, his voice muffled against the turned-up collar of his coat. "What? Eyes? Are you crazy? You stand around in the street looking for eyes in a window?"

Just the same, he stopped and looked up at the window I was pointing toward. "No," he said, shaking his head. "I don't see any eyes. Young fellow, you've got bats in your belfry." He walked quickly away.

I looked avidly through the snow-dusted windowpanes. A warmth pervaded my limbs. Exaltation, ecstasy poured through all my veins. The street lamps and the windows were enclosed in a mist of reflected light. Sleepily I walked over the cobblestones, but I did not see the eyes again. I concluded that I had been deceived, and I left the street.

At the movie theater half of the performance was over. The film was the same as before, the one with Eddie Polo in the chief role. I went backstage and waited for the first performance to finish. It wouldn't have done for me to start talking in the middle of the film, so I waited for it to end. I sat down on the step of a ladder that was leaning against a wall and closed my eyes.

The orchestra was playing some sort of waltz. The notes drifted slowly, lazily through the auditorium, then reached backstage and disappeared through the small window cut high up in the wall, through which the pearly brightness of snow falling into a hushed blue evening could be glimpsed. It was dark backstage. Seeping in through cracks, a weak red glow from the footlights scantily illuminated both ends of the stage. A feverishly stubborn mouse hastily tore at a bit of rotting wood, rolling and tossing it from one corner to another. A bored musician sang softly to himself:

In Berlin, in Ber-lin,
On the Kaiserallee . . .

I closed my eyes and thought of absolutely nothing. Emptiness absorbed me, embraced me, and poured a stream of fatigue over me.

The next morning I saw placards on the walls announcing "Final performance! Wrestling contests!" I gathered that the wrestlers would be leaving shortly. I read the placards one more time and noticed that the date of the farewell performance was yesterday.

Jason and Doli have probably gone, I thought. *Too bad I didn't get to say goodbye to them.* I walked through several streets. Then, as I came to one of the roads leading to the outskirts of town, I noticed three large roofed vans with small stout wheels. There were small signs hung on the vans: INTERNATIONAL CIRCUS. I watched the vans more closely and saw someone with a cigarette in his mouth at one of the windows. The features seemed to be Jason's. For something like a quarter of an hour I followed the vans. Then the window in which I had spotted Jason's head opened and I heard Jason's powerful voice calling me. I replied to his greeting. Then suddenly Jason disappeared from the window. An instant later the van stopped. Jason leaped through the opened door, ran toward me, and grasped my hand. "Keep me company for a while. We're on our way now to Pomerania, and from there to Germany—to Prussia." Then he complained at length because I hadn't come to see him, because I hadn't said goodbye.

I went inside the van.

Through a hole in the van Jason shouted to the man on the driver's seat, "Let's go!" The horses started off.

There were six people in the van besides Jason and me—three other wrestlers, Doli, and two female trick riders. The wrestlers sat on a torn mattress and played cards. The women were cooking some food over a camp stove. On the walls hung clothes and circus signs depicting the wrestlers in the arena in various embattled poses. The place was dark. A kerosene lamp shed a weak reddish light. Doli, covered with some sort of heavy old clothing, was sleeping on a straw mattress. The women—one of them tall and light on her feet, with black hair and firm large breasts; the other, an older woman, a blonde with a heavily powdered face—sat on the floor. The blonde had a cigarette in her mouth. The women spoke German to each other. When I came in no one paid the slightest attention to me, though the women looked me over. The wrestlers were busy with their cards, and Doli was asleep.

"You can sit here, it's soft," said Jason, pointing out a mattress. We both sat down. The van rattled, and the blonde held on to the camp stove to keep it from falling off its stool. The dark woman was telling her friend some kind of story.

"Do you get it? He came to me once—ha, ha, ha—that filthy wretch." She burst into a hearty laugh.

"So he wasn't as dumb as you said after all," the blonde replied, taking a puff on her cigarette.

At intervals one of the wrestlers shouted, "Two . . . seven . . . God damn it to hell!"

The lamplight fell on the wrestlers' heads, and their shadows trembled on the wall. Two of them were on their knees, and the third lay on his side on the floor. The place was warm from the heat of the massive bodies, which, in the narrow confines of the van, gave off a smell of healthy, well-muscled human flesh. The women now lay together in a corner, breasts and bellies pressed against each other, laughing loudly. Each time the van struck an uneven paving stone everyone shook and the money on the card table jingled. Whenever there was a particularly hard jolt one of the massive-chested wrestlers muttered, "God damn it to hell—again!"

"We're on the road once more," Jason said. "To tell the truth, your town's turned ugly for me. Never mind that it isn't particularly beautiful—nothing but factories and factories. But I never like staying very long in one place."

"How's Doli?" I asked.

"Who knows how he is? He's at death's door, but right down to last night's performance he's made his audiences happy. He has never once missed a performance." Jason got up and opened a bundle from which he took out a bottle of cognac. "You won't turn it down, right?"

I didn't reply. Pouring the cognac into a glass he had also taken out of the bundle, he handed it to me.

We both drank.

The van rattled and banged over the cobbles.

The card-playing wrestlers were getting more and more heated and passionate. Their thick bodies were in continual restless motion. The women lay pressed against each other, laughing into each other's faces as they told funny stories. The older one, the one with the cigarette in her mouth, emitted a cloud of smoke and, still gasping with laughter, cried "Ah, what a dumb goose."

The faces of the gamblers, now warm and flushed, could be seen in the light from the blue flame of the camp stove. The coins on the table never stopped jingling. Doli woke up, his blue eyes wide, his thin pale face covered with sweat.

"You ask where I would like to go?" Jason said. "It hardly matters to me. Sometimes here, sometimes there. What's the difference what country one is in? I forget the towns I've been in—like last year's snow."

Suddenly he laughed, grabbed my sleeve, and edged himself closer to me. "Do you remember the story I told you about the textile manufacturer's daughter? The night before last, when she read the placards announcing that we were giving our last performance in Lodz, she came running to my hotel and, as if absentmindedly, put a crisp hundred-dollar bill on the table. Then she flung herself into my arms, whispering sweet words—'darling,' 'beloved,' and other such tender expressions—in my ear. As before, I took the money and sent it to Doli. But, though I went to bed with that woman, I never stopped laughing—endlessly laughing. I actually laughed in her face. A strange woman; and I too was strange. A wrestler. A prostitute. That's certainly unusual. Ha, ha, ha." Jason's muscular body quivered when he laughed and made the floor vibrate. The betting money on the table laughed along with Jason as it danced and leaped about.

"Doli the clown, Doli, the sly, clever, quick-witted Doli, is going mad. He has no idea who is sending him such large sums of money,"

Jason said, still laughing. "He's been puzzling about the matter for several weeks now, and still hasn't the faintest cl. He believes it's a spirit that brings him the money, and he thinks therefore that nothing good can come from it. Doli's taken me aside in secret and, stammering, his voice trembling, has confided to me the story of the two hundred-dollar bills, and he's asked me what I think about it all, and who could have sent him the money. Finally he confessed that he was afraid to use it. The mystery that surrounds it keeps him from spending it. I told him not to be a fool—to find out whether the dollars were real or counterfeit and then to do with them what he thought was right. It was only with great difficulty that he allowed himself to be persuaded. Finally he sent off a hundred dollars to his sick mother in Prague, and he's using the other hundred to help heal his diseased lungs. Just the same, he goes about like a man in a madhouse trying to figure out the secret of the two hundred-dollar bills. Ha, ha, ha. Doli will go crazy." Jason's loud laughter resounded in the clattering van.

"It's strange enough to receive two hundred-dollar bills without having the least idea where or from whom they've come. Odder still when it happens in a town where one is a stranger and knows nobody," I said.

"Each time I see Doli taking a dollar out to change into Polish money," Jason continued, still shaking with mirth, "and see the helpless, desperate looks he casts at it, I start laughing again. Doli gives me a clown's scary look. 'Hey, fly-by-night with wrestler's muscles, why do you laugh?' If I keep on laughing, he says, 'You don't look like a donkey. I guess I was wrong.' Ha, ha, ha. You haven't heard any of Doli's jokes."

The card table jiggled, and there was the laughter of coins accompanying Jason's words.

One of the women acrobats, the dark one, stood up, straightened out her disordered dress, and ladled out several plates of soup. She called, "Caesar, Khvedo, Ketar, Jason, will you eat something?"

"No, no," said the card-playing wrestlers. "We ate our dinner in town."

"I won't have anything either. I too had my dinner in town," Jason said.

Only the women acrobats ate, crouched on the floor. They dipped their spoons slowly, leisurely into their plates, swallowing their soup as they continued their conversation. When they finished eating and had put their plates away, both women approached Jason. The blonde half-closed her eyes and, with an appreciative, secret sniff at his shoulder, said, "Jason, give us a drink." One of the women sat at Jason's left and the other at his right. They inched closer, pressing their lightly clad, supple upper bodies against his arms. Jason poured two glasses for them. They drank quickly, swallowing the cognac down at a gulp, then kneeling beside him, their dresses hiked up to reveal their slim, acrobats' legs, one of them said laughingly, "Jason, do you know how to keep from being bored as we travel?"

"Ah, Jason's nice," the other said, laughing.

They both pushed even closer to him. The smaller one with an impatient, feverish movement passed a hand through her hair, then put her head against Jason's and whispered something into his ear as she touched her rouged lips to his face. Then she drew her head back quickly, hid her face in her hands, and started to laugh as if laughter was gathered in her palms. The darker woman was instantly curious. Her face, with its sharp, impertinent nose, its thick brows over slightly protruding eyes, contracted as she demanded, "What did she tell you, the slut?"

All of a sudden the van gave a great jolt. The kerosene lamp shook, then fell from the wall. The place was almost dark. The two women uttered a loud and happy cry. The three wrestlers leaped to their feet inflamed and furious. Their eyes gleaming with gambling fever, they moved about nervously, impatiently, cursing a blue streak. In the dark, one could see their gigantic, fleshy bodies, their enormous heavy arms as thick as the bodies of children.

"Devil take it."

"Goddamned weather."

"A hell of a wind."

The driver, a questioning look on his face, poked his head through the opening into the van. One could see his red nose, hardened and weathered by winds and storms; his small dreary eyes, made tearful by the sharp air; and his small blond mustache. He called out something incomprehensible in the form of a question, then drew his head back. In a little while the lamp was relighted. Despite the steel hasps with which the metal floor was bound, the glass shade of the lamp had not shattered, saved by the wire mesh in which it was enclosed.

As soon as the lamp was relighted the wrestlers sat down and resumed their card game. The fracas that followed on the fall of the lamp had wakened Doli. His eyes wide, fearful, he asked, "What happened?"

He made a quick dance movement, then came to a stop. He stood there in his undershorts as if he was about to leap into the air. When the light came on and Doli was seen standing there in his shorts, the two women went off into gales of laughter which, though they held their sides, they were unable to restrain. "Ah, Doli. Ah, Doli."

Doli lay back down, covered himself with the covers, and looked around. He recognized me and, pressing my offered hand, he said, "How come you're here?"

I told him that Jason had invited me into the van.

I stayed in the van for another half hour. When I left, Jason and I embraced each other.

"Who knows? We may meet again," Jason said, looking into my eyes.

"Yes, if you've done it once, you'll do it twice," Doli said. "We'll certainly meet again."

I jumped down from the van. The two women gave my half-military clothing a perplexed, inquiring look. To the wrestlers, preoccupied with their cards, I was all but invisible.

26

A few days later the manager of the theater, his voice cold and aloof, said, "You know, there's been no increase in the paid admissions at the Venus since you started narrating, so I'm not going to be able to afford any extra expense."

I understood what he meant.

"Do I owe you any money?"

"Eighteen hundred marks."

He gave me the money and I left.

It was evening, around six o'clock. The town was clad in a white frost. There was no snow.

Where to go?

The dark glided over the sidewalks and paving stones on bare feet. I came to the main thoroughfare. Long files of pedestrians moved on both sides of the street. There was noise and laughter; there were lost fragments of words drifting in the air. The wheels of droshkys and tramways cut through an evening that dozed on its frost-covered cobblestones. Telephone and telegraph wires pulsed as if the town's living, blood-filled arteries were feeling the cold.

I had no place to go, so I went to the circus building. There were no lights in the windows. The circus was closed. Somebody had torn down the various placards, and all that was left hanging on the walls were a couple of gigantic feet, the last remnant of the lithographic color portrait of Bamboula the black wrestler.

I turned and left the circus without having any idea where I was going. I mingled with the stream of people and let myself flow with it. Off in the distance the electric lamps shone like radiant eyes. I went on. I felt the cold. The chill had no trouble reaching me through the lightweight clothes I was wearing. I went off to the sallow-faced Jew in whose home I had spent the previous night.

The moon peered down at the earth through silver hoops, as if into a well. The cold was light, caressing. A soft, silent night sailed through the air.

The sallow-faced Jew was standing before a wall and, with a piece of chalk in his hand, was doing sums of some kind, erasing and writing in whole columns of figures. He assigned a name to each of the numbers he wrote down.

"Seventy—Shlomovitch! Sixty-six—Fuchs. Two hundred twenty-five—R. Lazer's." He wrote only the numbers down. His hands were long, very long. His palms were wide; his shoulders, narrow; and his feet, small. He looked as if his entire upper body were controlled by his hands. As he wrote, his back was toward me. Seeing me, he turned for a moment, then went back to his writing. I bought a few bread rolls at the snack counter in the second room. A small girl with weak, filmed-over eyes and sickly red cheeks peered at the money and gave me change. I went into the dormitory room, lay down on my bed, and leaned back with my head clasped in my hands. It was dark here. The bright night looked in through the windowpanes. I thought I had done wrong in not asking Jason to get me into the circus as a laborer. Who could tell? They might have taken me on. Jason and Doli could have recommended me to the manager. Something might have come of it.

What would tomorrow bring? Or the day after? I had enough money to last for perhaps two days. I made a deal with myself not to buy any tea—to buy only bread with the money I had left. One could get free hot water at the train station. I would get a bottle and eat my meals at the station.

The door opened and the landlord came in. He took something out of the window and went back out. The door was left open, allowing the light from the other rooms to penetrate into the dormitory, where it shone on the walls. I started to count the flowers on the ceiling wallpaper. There were two hundred and ten of them. Then I counted the stripes on the walls. Later I shut my eyes and dozed. When next I opened them the clock was striking eight.

I went out into the street. I bought some more rolls and brought them back to my lodgings, where I asked the girl behind the snack counter to give me a bottle. When I got the bottle, I went off to the train station. There I filled my bottle at the faucet and ate my bread, washing it down with the hot water. Then I went back into town, where I wandered about in the streets until nearly eleven o'clock.

When I got back to my lodgings the landlord said that all the beds were taken and that there was no place for me to sleep. I left the boardinghouse and went back into town. The temperature had dropped, and I was cold. I returned to the train station, filled my bottle with hot water, and warmed my hands with it. I stayed in the station for half an hour. Then I left. A heavy snow was falling, and I was quickly covered with snow. I wandered about like this until dawn. I was blue with cold—nearly frozen stiff.

I sat down on some small steps near a house and tried to sleep. The cold would not let me close my eyes, and a wind devoured the clothes right off my back. I resorted to my old remedy: I started a conversation with myself. I asked myself questions and answered them. I kept my eyes closed and spoke sharply, lashing out at myself, not sparing myself the harshest words. Finally the pity of such self-torment reached me. I got to my feet and moved off at a swift pace to warm myself up.

All night long the snow fell, and the street lay under deep drifts of sparkling untouched snow. The grayness of dawn crawled over the enormous mounds, and sleep looked out of the windows of the houses. Sleepy, ill-rested workers carrying thermos flasks of coffee under their arms went toward their factories. The droshky drivers slept on their drivers' seats, and their horses blinked at the snow with their huge, sad, moist eyes.

At a street corner a couple of prostitutes approached, turning their pale faces and dejected eyes toward me. They talked, they shouted, they gesticulated, their bodies in constant motion. Their cries woke a droshky driver, who gave a pleased shout as he made a snowball and threw it at one of the women.

"Hey there, whores."

Both of the whores turned toward him. Standing where they were, they began to scold, flinging one sarcastic curse after another at him, like dogs who are afraid to bite but who stand in one place and keep on barking.

The droshky driver laughed at their curses. He opened his wide mouth and yawned hugely into the cold metallic air. A wizened middle-aged man began to extinguish the gas lamps. He greeted the droshky drivers as if they were old friends.

Among the passing workers I recognized several who had been frequent visitors to the Venus Cinema. I stopped one of them, a short Gentile with a thick gray mustache and plump unhealthy features.

"Is the strike over?" I asked.

"Yes. We've been at work for the last four days."

"Well, how much did you get?"

"Ten percent. Could have gotten more. Didn't have the strength to go on with the strike."

His voice was heavy, hoarse. He was still sleepy, and his years in the factory had taken their toll.

I went on. I recognized among the workers the man at whose house I had slept when I worked at the Venus Cinema. I stopped him and asked how things were. He cheerfully returned my "Good morning." He too said that they had been given a ten percent raise. He was a tall, merry fellow, some thirty-five years old, with large hands, a broad rough masculine face, a pair of ornamental mustaches, and lively small eyes. He complained because I was no longer narrating at the movie house. I told him I'd been laid off. He wondered how that could be and shook his head in disbelief.

I wandered about in the streets until nine o'clock. Then I went to visit Vogelnest.

27

I knocked at the door of Vogelnest's house. No one replied. Clearly there was nobody at home, so I went away. I bought some bread and went to the train station to have my breakfast. Now, for the third time, I noticed a pale, ragged, unshorn, bespectacled man with a gentle, weary look on his face, who, like myself, was taking water from the hot water tap. I made an attempt to strike up a conversation, but he didn't immediately respond. He listened to what I had to say, then turned away to put his bottle under the faucet. His white hands, with their slender delicate fingers, trembled. His head was buried deep in the collar of his coat, as if he was asking to be left alone and undisturbed.

"May I make your acquaintance?" I said. A withdrawn look came into his gentle face. Looking over the rims of his glasses, he let his eyes rest on me for a time, then turned his head away. He made an awkward movement with his foot that knocked his bottle, which was standing under the hot water tap, into the drain, where it shattered. He stood there, immobile, deeply discouraged, and stared at the bits of glass.

Turning to him, I said, "Would you like to use my bottle?"

Again he studied me over his glasses, giving me an earnest, inquiring look. Then, so softly that he could hardly be heard, he said, "But you eat first."

"No, I don't feel like eating yet. You take the bottle."

"I'll take it later, only after you've eaten."

I ate my bread as quickly as I could, then washed it down with some water, after which I handed him the bottle. He ate, then silently we went back into town.

"Are you from Lodz?"

"Yes," he replied quietly.

"What do you do?"

"Nothing. I'm not the only one. You know how it is."

"Where do you live?"

"In the Municipal Beggars' House." He smiled sadly.

Seeing my puzzlement, he added, "Don't worry, I'm not a beggar, even if I do live in the Beggars' House. And what about you?"

"Discharged from the army not long ago."

"Where do you live?" he went on.

The "Where do you live?" was asked in a tone meant to find out not where I lived but whether I had anyplace to live at all.

"Noplace."

He asked no further questions, understanding at once that my "Noplace" meant that I lived in the streets.

"How does one get into the Beggars' House?"

"You go to the municipality. To the Social Services Office, room number twelve. Make them give you a bed for a few nights in the Beggars' House because you've been evicted from your lodgings. No. You don't even need to say that. You tell them that you've just been discharged from the army. You'll show them a document to that effect, and with the greatest courtesy they'll give you a slip of paper and send you to the Beggars' House. The paper will entitle you to a bed for a few nights, but once you're there, you can get an extended stay. Yes, you'll find a place to sleep. A beggar can have a hard time finding space in the Beggars' House, but it's easy for a respectable man." He laughed. As he laughed, his face shrank, emphasizing his prominent cheekbones.

"Are there people like me among you?"

"Oh, a whole community. A commune in the Beggars' House. You won't be bored, *mein herr.* It's quite cheerful there." He laughed, screwing his pale transparent face into a grimace. He looked blue with cold.

We walked with light, quick steps. He was silent. Sometimes the wind tore a tatter from his ragged clothing.

After a few silent moments he turned to me. "You're not far from

• 152 •

the Municipal Building. Go on in. We'll see each other tonight in the Beggars' House." Then he left me.

I went into the Municipal Building and asked a functionary where I could find room number twelve of the Social Services Office.

"On the second floor," replied the functionary. I went to the second floor and entered room number twelve. A stout man was sitting beside reams of paper, writing something down with a pencil. For a while he ignored me, as if he had not heard me opening the door. I stood there for about a quarter of an hour before he looked up and noticed me.

"Can I help you?"

"I'm a demobilized soldier."

"There's nothing we can do for you," he said brusquely and turned his attention to his piles of paper.

"I'm sleeping in the streets."

He was silent.

"I'd like to have a permit to sleep in the Beggars' House."

He looked at me. "Documents?"

I handed him my discharge papers.

"You don't have a job of any kind?"

"No."

"Then how do you live?"

To that question I made no reply. He did not ask anything else. He wrote out a slip of paper and handed it to me.

"Good for five nights' lodging," he said, then buried his head once more in his reams of paper.

I left the Municipal Building, the bit of paper in my hand. I was tired from my long night's wandering through the streets. I was so sleepy I could hardly keep my eyes open. I walked through the dazzling snow with half-closed lids. I went to the Venus Cinema. The auditorium was open. The projectionist, who had only just arrived in the lobby, was testing a new film. Hardly paying any attention to me, he let me in, then locked the door. I went backstage, where I lay down on the bare floor and covered myself with my coat.

I was so worn out that I went right to sleep. It was late in the afternoon when I woke. It appeared to be almost evening. I went out into the lobby and tried to open the door. It was locked. There was no one in the theater.

I'll have to wait a couple of hours until they open the auditorium, I thought, then started pacing back and forth to keep myself warm. The chill of the bare floor had penetrated my bones, and I shivered. I left the lobby and went backstage again. There I noticed the window high up on the wall, and it occurred to me that it might prove to be a way out of the theater. I set a ladder that was standing there against the wall and climbed up to the small window and crept out. I found myself in the courtyard. I paused there for a moment, then went out into the street. For another hour and a half I wandered about the town. At dusk I approached a policeman and asked for the address of the Beggars' House.

"Sixty-one Rokotshin Street."

I didn't know where Rokotshin Street was, so I asked him. He gave me directions how to get there.

Rokotshin Street was on the other side of town. It took me nearly half an hour to get there. The Beggars' House was an old two-story building surrounded by a wooden fence. I rang the bell. The watchman, a Gentile in a white sheepskin coat, came out. I handed him my permit. He read it, then led me inside.

"According to the rules, you have to bathe first before you can be given a bed." Then he led me into a courtyard, to a low brick hut. When I had bathed, he took me back to the second floor of the main building, to a large room on whose door there was a sign that read SECTION ONE. Inside there were two rows of five beds each and a long wooden table that had been painted dark yellow. There were two old people lying in the beds. Both had had their heads shaved. One of them, a half-mad-looking fellow with an oval face, assumed a pathetic, pitiful look when he saw the two of us, myself and the watchman, come in. He blinked his slightly crossed eyes at us, then said in a foolish voice that was, just the same, long-practiced at plucking heartstrings, "A couple of pfennigs, please." Then he flung himself under the bedclothes and laughed delightedly, "Hee, hee, hee."

The other man was old. He was pale, swollen, closely shorn and shaved. He looked like a woman. He kept his eyes (over which there was not the least trace of an eyebrow) closed. He was stiff, as if frozen, and kept his head turned toward a window while he talked into the distance. He was half seated on the bed. His crooked legs stuck out from under the thin bedclothes, and he clung to them with his hands as if for support, to keep his bald head from falling back onto the pillow. His thin lips, like a couple of dirty white bones, opened and closed slowly, slowly, revealing two rows of short, rusty-looking teeth, as if rusty black nails had been driven into his blue gums.

Near the door, on a bench, sat a small, humpbacked fellow. He had a broad forehead and a massive round head sparsely fringed with white hair. His forehead was heavily furrowed, and the furrows were packed like ditches with deeply rooted dirt. Below that forehead his face was narrow, his cheeks sunken, his nose long, pointed, and crooked. Between his lips, pale as skin, his teeth showed, the upper row protruding like those of a dog. He had a wolf's long thin neck. His Adam's apple was thick, filthy, and protrusive, like a hardened swelling. He stood there, naked to his belly and bent in such a way that his hump stuck out high, like a strange load. He held his shirt in his trembling hands and, with hasty glances, searched it for lice.

"You pig!" the watchman shouted. "You'll go to jail for such filth!"

The hunchback raised one hand to ward off a blow; with the other he pressed his shirt to his hard, wrinkled, sunken belly, which had the look of decaying yellow leather. He bent his head and cried out in Yiddish, "Hey, dear *panyi*, dear sir. Don't kill me." The man in bed stuck his pointed head out from under the covers and rocked with laughter.

The thought that I would be living here struck me now with revulsion.

The watchman led me into the next room. A round-faced, snot-nosed, low-browed, narrow-chested boy of twelve with stunted hands and feet, such as idiots are born with, was crawling about the floor on all fours, using his hands like paws. He was puffing air through his cheeks and tossing his head like a goat being pursued by tormentors. There was a turbid look in his pale eyes. One of his upper eyelids was thick and overgrown, like an animal's. He stopped before a bed on which an aging Jew sat half dozing. In some acrobatic fashion the boy stuck his big toe into his mouth, then slapped his inflated cheeks with his fists and whistled at the dozing Jew in the bed.

The sleepy Jew opened one eye and gave the boy a slow look, then closed his eye again. Ten or twelve men dressed in thick, heavy clothing, all of it cut alike, like prison uniforms, stood around an iron stove built deep into the wall. Some of the suits they wore were so large that they dragged on the floor. The men pressed around the stove, gulping the heat in with their mouths, their hands and feet, their necks, their shoulders, their trunks. The scarlet red glow from the iron stove cast an unearthly dark light over the gazing faces, obscuring them, except for their sunken mouths, their deep-set eyes, and their uplifted noses. The men stood silently, bowed, holding their hands over the fire. They looked as if they were gathered about some corpse around whom candles were burning.

They looked around at us when we came in, turning only their heads, as if the sloth induced in their limbs by the coal heat had stiffened their bodies in place.

The boy inflated his cheeks and started popping them with his fists. Then, on his feet, he leaped toward me. Looking into my eyes, he called cheerfully, half speaking, half singing, "Baaah, baaah! Another one."

There was a fellow without feet standing on the windowsill. He wore a long beard that reached to his belly. His face was pale, wrinkled. In the deep grooves of his pale wrinkled face his skin showed yellow-white. He had a pipe stuck in his mouth. The pipe, in which no tobacco burned, was set in his toothless gums as if out of habit and was covered by his beard, the way grain in a field covers the entrance to a mole's burrow. Since he had no feet, he stood there held up by his large, thickly veined bony dark hands whose clawlike rapacious fingers were outspread like the tines of a pitchfork. Standing on the windowsill, he looked like a statue or a tombstone whose base, from great age, had crumbled or broken away.

The watchman took a key out of his pocket and opened a door. We entered a third room. Here for the most part were women. Old women. Several of them lay dozing in their beds. Others sat around tables or were gathered around the fire in an iron stove.

A lean sixty-year-old woman walked very slowly back and forth, talking to herself. Her hair had been cut like a man's, and her small head sat on her narrow shrunken shoulders as if it had been pasted on. She clasped her hands behind her reflectively and kept her dark wrinkled face averted from everyone. If one listened closely, one became aware that she was reciting *Minkha*, the first set of evening prayers. A woman in a wig, with a sickly, swollen pale face and eyes that looked as if gray glass had been set in their sockets, sat on a bench near the table, her head resting on her hands. She spoke to herself quickly, disjointedly. Scattered words reached me: "As you make your bed, so shall you lie in it. . . . That's what he wanted, so that's what . . . the knapsack didn't suit him, so now he . . . pluck him up by the roots . . . "

At the stove a woman with a paralyzed arm that hung at her side like the amputated wing of a goose was telling a story to a cluster of women who were jostling each other trying to get closer to the fire. On the floor near the window another woman sat apart from them all. It was hard to tell her age. Her face was yellow and furrowed, her nose reddened with constant cold. Her eyes were immobile and expressionless. From a distance one would think that she was very old, but when one approached her one could see that she was not as old as she had seemed. When she saw me and the watchman coming in, she crossed herself.

The watchman laughed. "D'you see her?" he said to me. "That

creature crosses herself every time she sees me. She thinks I'm an evil spirit who's responsible for her misfortune. What a good-for-nothing."

There were women also in the farthest room. All but one of them were standing around the fire. The exception lay in her bed and, with quivering pale fingers, was sewing something.

In the fifth room the watchman said, "There are empty beds here. You can have one of those two." He pointed at the beds and immediately left the room.

The room was very dark. The wall of a red brick building next door effectively blocked the sunlight from coming through the single window in the room. I was very tired. I lay down on one of the two beds and fell asleep at once.

I woke up at dawn at what must have been a very early hour, but because of the red brick wall there was no sunlight to be seen. There were five people lying in the nearby beds. I looked carefully at them and recognized the man whose idea it had been to send me here. His mouth was open, and his breath seemed to tear out of his chest in the constricted way that is a sign of unhealthy lungs. Under the hair of his unshaven face one could see his pale shrunken skin, which now, in sleep, had acquired a rosy tint.

Everyone was snoring cozily. Two of the sleepers had thin, gentle-looking features. The eyes of the others were sunk in their tormented faces.

Near the window were set some wooden panels on which various pictures (mostly the faces of beggars) had been painted. I recognized the picture of one of the beggars I had met in the first of the rooms I had come through. Evidently one of my neighbors was a painter. I was very curious to know which one it was, and I wished that one of the sleepers would wake up so I could talk with him and learn the identity of the painter.

The other room was noisy. There were sounds of people waking from sleep, moving about in their beds. A woman's apathetic, raw, dull voice reached me. It was a slow, lamenting, monotonic voice,

Modeh ani l'funekho, I thank Thee, O Lord. It was one of the beggars reciting the morning prayer. The words crept through the room and seeped into the walls.

Suddenly somebody near me stirred. The man lying beside me stretched his hand out and waved it about, as if fending something off. Then he woke, and his eyes sought the window, through which daylight was pushing its way.

"What's the wake-up time here?" I asked.

He looked at me and said, "Whenever you like. If you have something to eat in bed, you can lie here all day and all night."

"And the watchman doesn't get you up?"

"No. He doesn't care one way or the other about us."

"And there's no supervisor from the municipality?"

"I can't remember ever having seen a supervisor . . . the painter is really some snorer, isn't he?" he said, indicating the man sleeping three beds away from me. I recognized him as the fellow who had sent me to this place. "He can sleep that way two days and two nights running. And it's not because he's sick. He's not sick. It's just that he doesn't like to poke about in town. He'd rather lie here in bed and sleep. No, what am I saying? Sleep! He doesn't sleep. He lies there and stares. He just lies there and stares—two days in a row."

The man talking to me threw his covers off and jumped out of bed. He dressed quickly and went off into town. I too got up and went away. I wandered about all day and came back half frozen late in the evening. Everyone was already asleep except my neighbor, who sat beside the stove roasting potatoes that he had taken from his pocket.

I sat down beside the stove to warm myself. My neighbor was a dark, vigorous, hairy fellow with a lopsided face in which twinkled a couple of lively, merry eyes. He kept pulling bits of coal from his pocket and tossing them into the fire.

"Well, how goes it?" he asked with a smile as he burst the skins of the roasted potatoes.

I smiled back in reply. I liked him. He sat on the floor with his legs around the stove, looking like the Hebrew vowel point, *segol*.

"Have a couple of potatoes if you like," he said. There were no lights burning in the place. The fire in the stove cast a red glow. I sat down on the floor and accepted the roasted potatoes he handed me.

"The painter hasn't come back yet," he said, looking around. "It's almost certain that he won't come back today. He must have sold a picture somewhere, got his hands on some cash, and gone off to some dive to get drunk. He'll be back tomorrow and spend the next two days in bed." He threw several more bits of coal into the fire. "I worked in a factory unloading coal today and filled both pockets with coal. And let me tell you, I have *big* pockets." He gestured toward his pockets and showed me. There was a crackling in the stove, and the flames leaped up.

"How long have you been here?"

"Three weeks."

"And where were you before this?"

"In Warsaw, and there," he said, smiling, "there too I spent five weeks in a Beggars' House. I like big towns. One can always find someplace to sleep. In small towns, you know, you have to beg for a bed for the night. And if someone gives you a place to sleep, he looks at you suspiciously, thinking you'll steal something. In a large town, as you see, you just go to the Beggars' House. Though in Galicia, that doesn't work. There you have to have a packet of documents and papers, and everything has to be countersigned by the mayor. And I say to hell with all mayors. And that's why I don't go to Galicia.

"And what do you do?" he asked.

"Nothing."

"You mean, like me? No. You have some kind of job."

"Whatever comes my way."

"And if nothing comes your way for a long time, then you walk— or ride—to another town. . . . Well, eat some more potatoes. They're good."

Everything around us was warm. Our faces looked red in the light of the glowing coals.

"And how long can one stay here?"

"For months at a time. There's one fellow in this place who's been here for a whole year. But I think I'll only be here for a few more days. I'm thinking of going to Katowice. They say there's work there in the coal mines, expediting the cars. I'm tempted to go there, not so much because there may be work, but just to get away from here. There's always a catch to the stories about work. A couple of weeks ago there were rumors that there were jobs to be had in Danzig harbor. I had enough money for a ticket halfway there. So I walked as far as Torn, and from Torn I took the train right to Danzig. But there was no sign of any kind of work. There were thousands of unemployed Danzigers. And in addition to them there were thousands of unemployed Germans who had come to Danzig hoping to find work. So you see, it doesn't pay to go anywhere because it's rumored that there's work. And you," he said as he concluded, "how do you get on?"

I told him that I was a discharged soldier, and that I was unemployed.

"So things are bad for you and aren't likely to get better," he said, poking the red coals in the stove with a wire.

He started to doze. I took off my clothes and went to bed. For a few moments more my eyes rested on the fire in the stove and on the man on the floor dozing beside it. Little by little the fire died down until finally it went out. The man near the stove continued to sleep on the floor, his hands behind his head. Then he woke with a start, jumped to his feet, and went to his bed, where he lay down.

In the morning it was raining, a heavy winter rain mingled with snow. I went into town and came back almost immediately, rain-soaked and hungry. I had no more money for food. My dark neighbor was there. He sat beside the stove roasting potatoes. He invited me to eat. I did not refuse. I sat down on the floor—there were no chairs—and warmed myself.

"This sort of weather is frequent in Russia," the dark fellow said as he looked out the window. "Snow *and* rain."

"You've been to Russia?" I asked.

"Some distance into Russia. Actually, all the way to Siberia—and a bit farther on. As far as China, in fact."

Then, without asking whether I wanted to hear it, he began to tell a long and very strange story.

28

"You should know that I'm from Komarno, a small town in Galicia. In 1914 I was drafted into the army and sent to the front, where I fell into the hands of the Russians.

"If I had not made my escape one dark night, who knows whether I'd be talking to you now? It's eight years since I got away. In all that time . . . in all my wanderings I have not seen a single one of the two thousand German, Hungarian, Polish, Czech, Slovak, or soldiers of other nationalities who were with me in that filthy kennel of a prisoner-of-war camp fifteen versts from Vladivostok. I have reason to think therefore that most of them died of typhus and hunger. The story of my escape is not especially interesting. How I dragged on in the prisoner-of-war camp on the outermost border of Russia is a bit less boring, but not enough to make it worthwhile to recount it in detail.

"I still feel revulsion when I remember how the entire Fifth Royal and Imperial Austrian Regiment plodded drenched to the skin through muddy snow for two days and a night. We were all happy when a division of Cossacks encircled us and took us prisoner. All of us were happy except a Hungarian who kept crying, 'The Cossacks will shoot us. As I love God, the Cossacks will kill us.' The Cossacks not only did not shoot us, they gave us gifts of Russian cigarettes and bread. We in turn gave them German marmalade and chocolates. The terrified Hungarian quieted down. Things took a cheerful turn, and all of us sighed with relief because we were rid of our weapons and our lives were no longer in danger. But none of us had any inkling of the sort of trip that lay before us. Just think, the journey to the prisoner-of-war camp from Lemberg to Vladivostok would take us no less than four months. And that with hardly any rations.

"We were seven hundred and sixty-five healthy men. On that long journey we were only occasionally given bread and soup. The message, simply put, was, 'If you don't like it, die. We don't need you.' But, ingeniously, we outwitted death. In that appalling four-month ride to Vladivostok only two men died: a Czech and an overly refined Viennese. And they, God forbid, did not die of hunger but from a strange fever that even the doctor could not identify.

"As far as Kiev we traveled with Russian troops and were under guard. In Kiev there was a two-day delay. Here a special train with nine freight cars was ordered for us. We each received two loaves of fresh bread and a bowl of hot groat soup that warmed the freezing blood in our veins. Our guards were changed in Kiev, and there our regimental officer reminded us, 'Those of you who have Austrian money—better give it to me to exchange for Russian. No Russian peasant will take our money. We'll die of starvation on the way.'

"Austrian kreuzer and kroner poured into the hat he had taken from his head. He turned the money over to the commander of the Russian troops that would accompany us. A young sergeant-major with ruddy mobile features and small alert eyes. A Czech who knew a little Russian served as translator. He told the sergeant-major what was needed. 'Good,' he said. He was going into town and would change the money and bring back provisions.

"No sooner said than done. He took one of the guards with him and was off.

"A little while later, those of us who had been sitting in the lower level of our freight car could see a wagon some distance away coming toward us. A bearded Russian driver sat on the front seat along with the sergeant-major. Their heads were in constant motion, and the driver kept spitting on both sides of the wagon. When they neared the train, the sergeant-major leaped down from the wagon and shouted, 'Four men for a work detail.'

"Four prisoners climbed down from the train. Only then did we see that instead of a load of provisions, the sergeant-major had brought back a wagon load of the most dreadful Russian liquor.

"We dared not say a word. After all, we were in their hands. A shudder swept over us as we realized that for the whole of our long journey there would be no bread. Only liquor. We clenched our teeth and kept still.

"The sergeant-major cleared one of the cars of prisoners and stored the liquor in it. The men were shoved into other cars.

"All this unloading and loading of liquor took place half a verst from the station. Once en route the sergeant-major came to terms with the engineer. Guards were set to look after the liquor, and the train rolled.

"In no time at all the guards were dead drunk. Even the engineer could hardly stand on his feet. One of the Russian soldiers, seeing the engineer drunk, shouted for the sergeant-major, who came running. Tearing his hair, he shouted at the reeling engineer, 'You'll run the samovar into a river. You son of a bitch. Just wait,' he yelled. 'We'll sober you up.'

"He ordered two of the soldiers to strip the engineer. 'You scum, you. Filling your pig's gut with drink. You want to kill us all? You want to drive the train into a ditch? Never mind, little brother. We'll sober you up quickly enough. I'll drive the alcohol from your belly. I'll give you a clean head in a minute.'

"When the engineer resisted being undressed, the sergeant-major shouted, 'Stop that clawing.' Then, *pow!* he threw a right to his nose.

"The frost burned and shimmered like a rainbow. One's breath froze. Cold! It was fearfully cold! The wind scattered sharp needles into the air.

"Within minutes the engineer was mother-naked. The frost made his rosy skin look like that of a dead goose. His face turned blue and rigid in the cold. His muscles contracted. Little mounds of flesh quivered here and there on his vigorous body. 'Take his hands,' the sergeant-major ordered. The two soldiers promptly grabbed the engineer's blackened, work-worn, callused hands.

"'And you'—the sergeant-major turned to two other soldiers—'you two take his feet.' The soldiers did as they were told. The engineer, his head between a soldier's feet, bellowed and wept. A thread of black slobber and gobbets of vomited food hung from his mouth.

"'One, two, three,' counted the sergeant-major. 'Heave!' With all their strength, the soldiers flung the naked engineer two meters off into the heavily encrusted snow.

"The sergeant-major went up to him. 'That's it. That's it, little brother. There's the bath to sober you up.'

"The engineer was indeed sober—and terrified. His head bobbing up and down, he yelled, 'Help!' There was no reply. The drunken guards slept like the dead. Again the engineer yelled, 'Help!' then babbled, 'God keep me from what could happen if anyone came by and found us drunk on duty. Four years in the pokey. Four years!' He went off, leaping from one car to the next, shouting wildly as he went, 'Four years! Four years!', until finally he made his way back to the engine.

"At five o'clock in the morning the train stopped at P. There the engineer and the fireman were relieved. By now the guards were sober. The sergeant-major himself kept a watch on the liquor to make sure no one else would get drunk. By six thirty he was on the floor. But drunk though he was, he was faithful to his duty. He lay sprawled across the doorway, a pistol in his hand, warning repeatedly, 'Anyone dares to take a bottle gets a bullet in his head. I'm not getting any four years in jail for you sons of bitches.'

"The train sped across fields, rivers, valleys. At lunchtime it stopped again. The sergeant-major came running to our officer. 'Damn it to hell, the liquor's driving me crazy. You take it back. It'll keep your spirits up, little brothers. Anyhow, it's enemy loot.'

"There were more than eighty bottles left. In no time at all the seven hundred of us had emptied the bottles, setting aside two to give to the new engineer. A couple of hours later a desperate sergeant-major was back again. Gesticulating wildly, he cried, 'There's big trouble ahead. The new engineer is dead drunk. He's going to run you into the Black Sea. The dog! I'll teach him to be drunk on duty.'' He was beside himself with rage.

"The liquor had stirred us up, roused the blood in our sleeping limbs. The freight car was deafening. People spat, quarreled in German, Hungarian, Czech, Slovenian. Fights broke out. The car was thick with stinking human vapors.

"Suddenly the train stopped in the middle of a snow-covered field. For miles around there was not a footprint to be seen. We got out of the cars and stretched our legs. All at once loud shouts were heard at the front of the train.

"I climbed into the locomotive to see what was up.

"The sergeant-major and two soldiers were tearing the clothes off the new engineer, a corpulent, thick-necked Russian. The sergeant-major kept pounding his cheeks, his neck, and his belly. When the engineer was naked, they lifted him up and threw him like a ball into the field. One could hear the sound his body made breaking through the crusted snow. The ice sent up a groan into the vast silence. For a second the engineer's heavy body, now red and blue, gleamed on high in the full light of the sun; then it sank into the snow as into a grave.

"'Holy Jesus!' A sputtering, hoarse voice rose above the steppe and was carried away without echo across the dead distances of the white fields. Then silence. The snow buried the naked man so completely that he disappeared.

"The soldiers on the train laughed coarsely, spitefully, and the sergeant-major encouraged them. 'Well, my lads. Will the son of Satan be sober now?' His stocky body shook. 'After a bath like that his belly will be as purged as the apostle Paul's when he fasted for Christ's soul. His head will feel lighter. The bastard son of a donkey will know that snow is white and won't drive us into the Black Sea. The son of a bitch. Ha, ha, ha.'

"Minutes later two of the soldiers dragged the engineer out of the snow. He was red, his face suffused with blood, his eyes open, blinking and squinting like a man who has just waked up and cannot bear the too bright rays of the sun. He didn't know what had happened to him, where he was, or why he was being hauled about. It was clear from the staring, foolish look on his face that his mind was a total blank and that he was now thinking what to think.

"He snuffled and tried to clear his throat. Then, smelling the odor of liquor in his mouth, he asked in a plaintive and childish way, 'I beg you. Won't someone give me a little drink?'

"Those were his first words. There was a plug of crusted snow clinging to one of his large, mud-smeared feet, but he didn't feel it. One of the soldiers knocked it off with the butt of his rifle.

"Back on board the train a couple of soldiers started to rub him down, kneading his flesh like dough. Then they set him before the fire of the huge boiler of the locomotive. The engineer came to and smiled apologetically. 'Ah, some bath you gave me.' He dressed guiltily, quickly. Minutes later the train was in motion.

"The sergeant-major came into the car where our officer was. He gave him cigarettes and chatted with him with the help of the Czech who understood Russian. He didn't salute him but instead treated him like a man on the same level as himself, calling him, 'Comrade Lieutenant.' As he talked, he drew slowly, thoughtfully on his cigarette, keeping it more often in his hand than in his mouth—as if he were smoking not for the smoke's sake but because things were boring, dreary, dull. In short, he smoked like a real officer. The lieutenant, meanwhile, kept smiling into the sergeant-major's face.

"On the second day of the trip we had no more bread left and were beginning to get hungry. The sergeant-major was told by the fireman that it would be two days before the train reached a central military depot where supplies for prisoners *might* be found.

"His manner as he recounted this to our officer was hesitant, mournful, dismayed—as if he was our best friend, our provider. He bowed his head penitently and waited to hear what the Czech would say. He stood musing; then, perking up, he said, 'Never mind, brothers.' He spoke to the Czech, but his words were meant for our officer. 'God won't let us starve. We'll figure something out.'

"Then he described his plan.

"All the prisoners would be divided into squads of twenty men each. Each squad would choose two men. At each village these two would be sent out to collect food from the peasants. That was how it had to be. There was no other way.

"Quickly the squads were formed. Each squad elected its two leaders. When everything was ready, the sergeant-major stuck his head out of the first car and shouted, 'Comrade Lieutenant!' The Czech who understood Russian plucked our officer by the sleeve to indicate that he was being called. Our officer went to the door (there was no window).

"'Well?' inquired the sergeant-major.

"In a resounding bass our officer flung the word 'ready' into the air.

"'*Uzjeh*.' The Czech, like an echo, sounded the Russian word for 'now.'

"The sergeant-major turned his head to the other side and shouted an imperious, 'Hey! Engineer!'

"The engineer poked his head out. 'What, Comrade Sergeant-major?'

"'Stop your samovar,'' the sergeant-major shouted. The engineer understood, and the train stopped at once.

"'Squad leaders out of the car,' our officer commanded. Some seventy men pushed their way through the crowds and leaped down from the train.

"The officer, the sergeant-major, and the engineer went into a huddle. The engineer pointed to something on his right. Nearby there were some low, snow-covered hills between which we could make out some dark glittering squares. They were peasants' huts in a village.

"The sergeant-major shouted, 'Seventy knapsacks.' Seventy knapsacks were thrown out of the car. The sergeant-major spoke for another minute or two. Then our officer commanded his seventy men, 'Fall in! To the left, march!'

"And the seventy men, including myself, turned off onto a snow-covered path. We moved away from the stopped train and approached the village. At the head of the column were the sergeant-major, our officer, and the Czech who spoke Russian.

"We moved silently, sliding about in the untrodden, knee-deep snow. As we neared them, we looked curiously at the white, snug little peasant huts.

"An old peasant woman, catching sight of us at twenty paces, was frightened half to death. Our foreign faces, our Austrian uniforms terrified her. She stood petrified, openmouthed, staring at us. Suddenly she began to run toward the village, wringing her hands and yowling. On her way she met a peasant wearing a sheepskin hat drawn down over his ears. It appeared that the peasant asked her what was the matter, because she shrieked as if one of her pigs had perished and cried, 'Don't ask, Matvei. Don't ask what happened. Oh dear me, disaster for the Russian people. The Germans have taken Moscow. They're here. Among us. In our village.'

"She took a deep breath, pointed at us, then ran desperately on, screaming the news all the way that the Germans had taken Moscow. The second peasant looked us over, crossed himself, stuck out his tongue, then ran off like a ghost on his long legs.

"The Czech and the sergeant-major laughed and explained to our officer what the peasant's words and gestures meant. Our officer said in German, 'Yes. The Russians are an oxlike people.' This, the Czech translated as, 'Yes, the officer says that Russian women are foolish but Russian men are wise.'

"The sergeant-major agreed. 'It's true. Russian women are the most foolish in the world.'

Now the sergeant-major turned thoughtful. His low brow was wrinkled; his small eyes glistened. To the Czech he said with a sly smile, 'Tell your officer to keep his men here.' Without waiting for the man to translate, he signaled a halt. We stopped.

"'If the peasants think you've taken Moscow, you'll have an easier time getting bread. That being the case, little brothers, let two of the men go to the magistrate and demand that he hand over two hundred loaves of bread.'

"The Czech translated all this to our officer, who wondered how such a clever notion could have entered into the head of a stupid Russian.

"The scheme worked. The Czech and one other man went to the magistrate and asked for two hundred loaves of bread. The village was a large one, almost a small town, and it was not hard to collect two hundred loaves of bread from the peasants. The bread was loaded onto a ladder-sided peasant wagon. The sergeant-major shouted to the driver, 'To the train tracks, march!'

"Some twenty minutes later the train was in motion.

"The story was repeated at the next village, but since it was smaller, we only got a hundred loaves. In the third village we got eighty loaves. By the time evening rolled around we had a thousand loaves of bread on the train.

"One thousand eight-pound peasant loaves (the lightest weighed five pounds)—well-kneaded, well-baked, dark loaves—found in such a windswept lonely place. It was a dream. A tale out of *The Thousand and One Nights*.

"We sang and danced for joy. A thousand loaves. We caught the sergeant-major up and lifted him high. Our lieutenant, tears in his eyes, gripped the sergeant's hand and presented him with his gold watch. The sergeant-major turned his head aside and at first would not accept the present. But then he heard the Czech's translation of our officer's speech: 'All seven hundred of us who are here are convinced that you've saved our lives. We will not forget this Russian officer to our dying day. We beg him to accept this small present as a token of our gratitude.' At these words, particularly at the use of the word 'officer,' which the Czech translator had thrown in as his own gift, the sergeant-major blushed and allowed himself to be persuaded. He accepted the watch. With a wise shake of his finger, he said, 'Tomorrow there will be more.'

"The sergeant-major kept his word.

"The next morning when there was no real daylight yet and the Russian fields were still enveloped in a frosty darkness, the sergeant-major's hoarse shout was heard shattering the dawn: 'Hey, engineer. Stop your samovar.'

"And we, our seventy men, went for bread once more.

"That same evening we had two thousand five hundred loaves in our possession. Imagine! Two thousand five hundred. At lunchtime the brains among us had counted five hundred. Two hours later, nineteen hundred. Finally, twenty-five hundred. A mighty number, achieved little by little.

"But it would seem that that still wasn't enough for the sergeant-major. He was seized by a real bread compulsion. He kept his head stuck out of the car. The keen wind, smelling of the steppe and of frost, whipped his sunburned face as his clever eyes scanned the horizon for villages that might be lurking there. He was like a card player watching for money. He could spot a village kilometers away, though the whole landscape as far as the eye could reach was entirely a sea of snow. His head bobbing happily up and down, he put two fingers into his mouth and sent a whistle toward the frozen sky, then shouted, 'Hey engineer! Stop your samovar.'

"And we pulled the same trick again. Entered the village armed. Talked German among ourselves. Spread the news that the Germans had taken Moscow. No doubt the sergeant and the guards could have been shot for this game, but it all went smoothly.

"For three months we wandered about in this fashion until we arrived in Siberia at a gigantic prison camp that had in it a hundred captured Austrian and German soldiers. They led atrocious, ghastly lives. I could see that there was no way to survive in that place, so I made my escape.

"I reached Vladivostok, the Russian port city, and hung about, doing nothing. I survived on what I occasionally earned carrying baggage to the port or to the train station. One day as I was idling about in town, my hands in my pockets, I was approached by a small, sly-looking Japanese named Hamata. He looked me over and went on. I thought he was an informer who would turn me over to the Russian authorities. Though the penalty for escaping from the camp was not severe—at most ten days in jail—I tried to avoid that district for a while. It was not the penalty that mattered; what counted was being back in that camp. Remembering how horrid it was gave me the shivers. A couple of days later I met the canny Japanese swindler again. This time he stopped me.

"'What are you doing here?'

"'Nothing.'

"'Are you a Jew?' the Japanese asked, looking intently into my face. I could not understand why he wanted to know. Though I was frightened, I replied, 'Yes, I'm a Jew.'

"The Japanese noticed that I was afraid. A sly smile appeared in his froglike face. 'Nothing to be afraid of. I'm no cop. Though,' he added, 'I can behave like a cop if you don't do what I tell you.'

"Still frightened of him, especially because he was speaking German, I said, 'What do you want?'

"'I don't want you to do me any favors. I have a business proposal that will make us both rich.'

"'Business with me?' I shrugged. 'Can't you tell that I haven't a groschen to save my soul?'

"'You can keep your money. For the business I have in mind I don't need your money. I'll advance whatever little cash the project needs.'

"'Then what do you want of me?' I asked.

"'Don't worry. I'm no cannibal. A man like you who has, as it were, been cast up here should know that. We Japanese are not people eaters. I'm talking about a scheme that will make us both rich. But you have to understand business, *mein herr.* Everything depends on that.'

"'All right. Tell me what's needed.'

"'Before I tell you what the scheme is, you have to answer one question. And don't let it surprise you. I'll explain in a moment why

I have to ask it.' He stepped closer and said, 'Are you circumcised?'

"I stopped in my tracks, crimson with rage. I felt like punching him in the face. I thought I was dealing with one of those people who hang about big cities looking for sacrifices to their criminal lusts. The Japanese evidently guessed what I was thinking. 'First of all, there's no need to let my question upset you. You're a soldier. Such words aren't new to you. Furthermore, *mein herr*, you're an escapee. Don't think for a moment that I don't know. Finally, you're making a big mistake if you think I asked you that question because . . . because . . . I want to . . .' Here he spoke a certain word.

"I stood awhile in thought. Then he asked me to go into a coffee house where he would explain what he had in mind. I went with him.

"'Here's how it is. If appearance means anything, you have the look of a true racial Jew. In China there's a huge region whose inhabitants are Christian converts. They are very devout Christians and know the Bible exceptionally well. The fools think of them-selves as very sinful. And they regard a Jew, a real Jew, as the holiest of men. In Peking, indeed, there is a small cluster of Jews, but they're not really Jews. They're Chinese, with Chinese facial features, and are the same sorts of fools. I'll take you with me to the region where the Christians live. There I'll put up a tent and send out placards announcing that a real circumcised Jew, a true great-grandson of Jesus Christ, has come and is dispensing remedies. Do you under-stand the scheme? There's no swindle in it; it's all according to law and truth. Isn't it true that you are a Jew? And aren't you, therefore, the grandson of Jesus Christ?'

"I laughed at the strange plan—and agreed to do it.

"'You'll be paid a certain sum for each remedy. Obviously, the more the better. As soon as we make our pile we'll go off to Japan, where I can get a passport made for you and you can go on to America.'

• 173 •

29

"In the morning, Hamata, the Japanese, took me to a store where he bought me a new suit. Then we boarded a ship from which we debarked on the coast of China. For several days we traveled through watery rice fields until we reached the district in which we were supposed to become millionaires. It was indeed a district where the fanatical Chinese Christian converts lived. The Japanese pitched a tent for me and put up a couple of wooden placards that said, in unabashed Chinese and English script, 'A real Jew, the grandson of the Holy Ghost and Jesus Christ! Newly arrived for limited appearances. A veritable circumcised Jew. Will prescribe remedies for the infirm, the crippled, and for those in spiritual pain. Every second day, psalms will be read in Hebrew, the language of our father Moses, Jesus Christ, King David, and the prophet Joshua.'

"Ah, what a head that Japanese speculator had on him! He told me that he had been a student in Berlin, where, on Grenadier Street, he had had a Jewish mistress. He had traveled everywhere. Even to Warsaw and to Lemberg.

"And do you think for a moment that the disgusting business he had concocted with me didn't succeed? Every day thousands of Chinese came to me. They told me their troubles and begged for my help.

"I can't help laughing when I recall the times that I stood behind a red tabernacle cloth that Hamata had had made for me; and how the Chinese Christian fanatics fell on their knees and prayed to me for help. Still, there was much about that first 'season' that filled me with revulsion. It was morally degrading and insulting to my sense of human decency.

"But I thought, 'Survival is everything. Too bad. I have to submit to the destiny that Hamata holds in his hands.'

"Hamata sat in a little anteroom and collected money from each of the Chinese, to whom he handed a bit of paper with a cross on it—a sort of admission ticket to my presence.

"The placards said, 'Every second day, the grandson of the Holy Ghost will read psalms in Hebrew.' And every other day thousands of Chinese gathered in the huge arena in which I stood on a raised platform and recited—no, not psalms. I sang songs from Lemberg Gimpel's Theater. 'Lekho dodi' and other songs. I sang no psalms for the reason that, first of all, I didn't know a single complete psalm by heart. And second, given my strange, miserable, and degraded situation, I didn't want to risk disgracing the Bible in any way. Hamata couldn't care less whether I sang songs from Gimpel's Theater or the passages from the Psalms which he had promised but about which he knew nothing at all. He sat by the cash box and sold tickets.

"We stayed in that district for several weeks, and I'm sure that by then Hamata had acquired a couple of thousand dollars. Then we left the district to go to another. And there we met our downfall.

"One fine sunny day a group of Chinese policemen led by a mandarin showed up and arrested me. I learned that the Japanese had shown a clean pair of heels—had disappeared with every penny of our earnings. I was left behind without a cent, in a Chinese prison.

"I was in that prison for more than half a year. What I suffered there is beyond description.

"After six months I came to trial. The Chinese judges did not know rightly how to punish me. They were not Christians. Like most Chinese bureaucrats, they were Taoists and unwilling to meddle in Christian matters. To avoid offending the French and the English, they decided to send me to the central court in Peking. In that court I was charged with extortion. But the court ruled that I had not really broken the law. I was a Jew and a Christian. Why might I not be a grandson of Jesus Christ in the same way that any devout Chinese could regard himself as a grandson of Confucius or of Lao-tse, or as a devout Hindu might be called Buddha's grandson, or a Mohammedan could think of himself as a grandson of Mohammed? As for taking money for giving remedies, they concluded that holy men did that sort of thing.

"The Chinese judges were as wise as they were brief. And I was freed.

"Now, if I liked, I could go searching for Hamata and try to get my money back. But I had no hope of catching him anywhere.

"I went to the Austrian ambassador in Peking and explained how I had gotten there. How the Japanese had threatened to turn me over to the Russian military, and how he had brought me to China. From the Austrian consulate I received money and documents meant to get me back to Vienna.

"But I did not go back to Austria. What would have been the point of traveling all that distance only to put on Austrian army pants again?

"I went to Switzerland instead. Only when the war was over did I go back to my home in Galicia. My parents were no longer there. They had died in an epidemic at the time of the siege. I have no regular line of work, and I move about, as you see, from town to town, looking for whatever I can get."

30

He set his shoes down carefully. Then, with weary lassitude, he put his hands behind his head and got ready to doze.

"Listen, I want to go job-hunting with you to Katowice. What do you think?"

"I'd be very pleased," he said, his eyes still closed as he stretched his legs more vigorously toward the stove.

We agreed that we would go on foot to Katowice. When he was fully asleep, I got up and went into town.

I made my way once more to Vogelnest's house. I knocked on the door. Mrs. Vogelnest opened it. There were marks of tears on her pale, transparent face. Her eyes were swollen and red. Evidently there had been some kind of misfortune. I did not have the courage to inquire, but she herself told me what had happened.

"My husband is dead, you know."

I stood stock still, astonished. She said nothing more, but resumed weeping into her white handkerchief as she handed me a newspaper. I scanned it for news of her husband. It was easy to find. There, in a short column, was written the news that one Viktor Vogelnest, thirty-two years old, had committed suicide by throwing himself under a train.

I was silent. She put her coat on, then turned to me. "If you have time, perhaps you could do something for me."

"Please."

"Stay here. Vogelnest's relatives will undoubtedly be coming. And I have to leave."

"Very well. I'll stay."

Quickly she left the apartment.

I was left in it alone. None of the beds had been made. There were various papers scattered all over the table.

I sat down next to the window and looked out at the rain-filled sky that hung like a dark weight over the town. An hour went by, then another. Nobody came. The place was quiet, very quiet. It was beginning to be dusk. I had no money. Hungry and weary, I lay down for a while. I slept hard yet restlessly. I woke at four. I searched for and found a key. I locked the door and went out into the street. The weather was dry and cold. The street was covered with gleaming ice.

Where to go?

I wandered about for some three hours, then went back to the apartment, where I took off my clothes and tried to go properly to sleep. My head ached, and I was neither fully awake nor asleep. My eyelids were heavy, and I felt the descending dark pasting itself on my eyes.

I woke at four in the morning. There was a noise like a rain of flies in a nearby room. It was some sort of machine just starting up. Out in the corridor sounded the bustle of people who are driven to get up early by the jobs to which they are harnessed.

Unable to sleep any longer, I got out of bed and got dressed. Because it was still dark, I lighted the lamp. I began to think about the unhappy Vogelnest, and it seemed to me that I had had dark premonitions about his death for some while now. Surely I had sensed—given his fragmented speech and the way he staggered when he walked—that he was not meant to live.

Since I had nothing else to do, my eyes settled on the scattered papers on the table. When I moved them about with a finger, I noticed several sheets covered with nervous handwriting. I began to read. As I read, I trembled. I felt my soul overmastered by a boundless yearning that seeped into my being like some sweet, sharp poison. It was a yearning for the eternal death which frees us from earthly suffering. At the same time I was conscious of the music surging in the words, which made the yearning even more tender, more intense.

What was written was in the form of an unbound, unfinished narrative. The passion for death seemed to peer out of the words with that delicate beauty one sees in the eyes of a sick child. I read:

THERE

Once, as he made his leisurely way back from the fields and started up to his apartment on the first floor, he was met on the stairs by a young woman with wild blazing brown eyes who barred his way. She gazed at him, then wept without saying a word.

He stood a couple of steps away from her and enfolded her in a glance from his unmoving, pale eyes. He too was silent as he kept his eyes on her.

They stood near each other for a long time, both of them

immobile, until in a tearful voice she called, "Louis! Is it you?"

Imperceptibly he trembled. His hands moved briefly, and a flame stirred in his sad, quenched eyes. "Come," he said, and went into his apartment. She followed. Once inside, he sat near the table, while she took a chair that stood beside the window. Facing him, she gazed at her long white hands, now folded in her lap. He did not look at her. He kept his face averted, looking at a small, half-erased picture on the wall.

Suddenly she raised her eyes feverishly to his and, speaking hastily, said, "Do you want me to stay? If not, I'll go." She started to rise. He got to his feet quickly and barred her way. His voice deeply tender, he said, "Miriam!"

She resumed her seat and looked lovingly at him.

... As silently as thieves, entire days slipped away on those roads that lead to infinity; and each day took with it whole treasures of silence from the diamond of sorrow.

All who are silent love the storm; and our pale mother died when the storm flung waves of rain into the world's face, striking it blind. Our pale, white mother saw death wandering the roads and pitied him and called him into her house. And death kissed our pale mother's eyes and breathed his breath into her soul saying, "Come to my country."

And our pale mother let fall a silver tear and replied to death, "How can I go to your country, since I am the mother of all those in the world who are silent? Since I am the mother of every mute soul?"

Then death shook his curly black hair and replied to our pale mother, "Do but look at my country and you will see that your bit of world is as a tear by comparison with it; and you will see how many pure, mute souls wait there for a good and saintly mother; how many souls that formerly endured the agony of their gray lives now yearn for your pure and tender hands."

... Thus she wrote and gave it to him to read. Often, when he read what she had written, an unperceived tear rolled down his face. He kissed the writing on the page and stood there weeping. And when sometimes a sunbeam in search of purification lost its way and stumbled onto that page, the tear radiated a few thin threads taken from the network of the rainbow, and together they went off into the world in search of purification.

Days paired with days gave birth to new days—and died.

They lived together. Louis felt himself fused with Miriam. And the more intimate they felt themselves to be, the more intense and encompassing was the autumn in which they walked, and the more densely woven was the silence that breathed from their eyes.

Sorrow and silence are always the same. And sorrow draws one to eternal silence.

Often when the autumnal one walked in the meadow with his sister a pale blue evening enfolded the bosom of the earth with gold-spun wool from the setting sun. From the blue sky melancholy, yearning star-eyes shed a dewy sadness on their heads. Then an insubstantial, light form trembled above the grasses, trembled and bent and swayed back and forth, and a strange feeling settled in their hearts. And Miriam said to Louis:

"Something's drawing me home."

"Where is your home?"

"Where is my home? Perhaps somewhere where the sky kisses the earth. Perhaps there where the blue fabric of the sky comes to an end."

She lowered her eyes and sat pensively. Every so often, deep in thought though she was, she looked about at the world; and her silence grew increasingly sad and tender.

And thus she went about, listening to the breezes in the meadow rolling about like mischievous children pursuing a poor dried leaf, which had breathed out its springtime soul last year; tossing it into the air, as if they meant to drive it to heaven, to the silver seeded clouds; then, with a laugh, letting it lie between a couple of grasses, only to resume their teasing of other dried leaves.

He felt a pang in his heart each time she uttered the word "home." He was overwhelmed with the sense of a dear familiarity more intense than anything he had ever felt before. Though he did not clearly understand what the word "home" actually encompassed, still it struck a note on that small, silent, interior violin that resided in his soul. A note, and then that violin began to play, and a wordless melody gushed in him, and one sound escaped into the wide, wide world: *home.*

And Miriam's passionate glances enfolded him and said, "You know, brother, that the world is large—very large; and yet though you may go through highways and byways, you will never find home. Because home is not in this world."

Once when he came into the apartment he found Miriam's notebook lying open on the table, the pages closely overwritten with her wild, sinuous handwriting.

On this pale evening I went in, and a shadow-braided darkness flowed into my longing eyes. The wind unbound my hair and wished to unite my locks with the night. I went out and looked up at the star that calls to me. All at once I saw standing before me that insubstantial, light form which, like a brother to our shadows, wandered after us when the world's sorrow bathed our souls. For a while I was frightened. My pulse surged more quickly, as if a wave of blood had crashed against the wall of my heart. He held his cold bony hands out to me, and I felt a sense of intimacy with them, an intimacy that immediately radiated from my eyes to his.

"Sister, I am called Death," he said, and from his countenance there emanated a sense of peace that came from a world that no one has ever yet trod. "I am called Death, and to all those who are born alienated into this world and who lose their gray days in alienation I show a home, and I prove a loyal father to them. And are you willing to go with me to that long-yearned-for home? Close your eyes and follow me silently. Hush, hush . . . just like this . . . quietly.

When he finished reading he felt as if some intimate element in his heart had been torn away forever. Almost at once the sense of emptiness he had felt in his soul intensified, and he was oppressed by the feeling that his sister Miriam would never come to him again.

I stopped reading. A sweet rustling noise sounded in my head, as of voices suddenly heard coming from windows one passes when walking through dark side streets late at night.

I looked at the scrawled handwriting. It was a thin jagged script that made me think of needles whose points were set in blood. I looked around the room into which the dark had now crept through the window like fog on one of those autumn days when the muddy hours, cold and wet, and in splattered canvas shoes, drag themselves slowly in from the roads like drenched cats looking for cozy corners in which to doze.

At ten the next morning Vogelnest's wife came in. She said nothing, but maintained the silence of a woman who carries misfortune in her limbs like lead. Though she moved about, it was as if she saw nothing, looked at nothing.

She walked quietly in and sat down next to the table as if waiting for something. Sitting there, she looked like a hungry child who is angry at everyone and yet, too embarrassed to ask, waits to be given something to eat. Half an hour passed that way, without words.

Then she lifted her clear, childlike, melancholy eyes and smiled lovingly, tenderly at me. A mother's smile. As if she were sixty years old and I all of ten.

I was surprised and confused.

She smiled sadly. Then she spoke slowly, almost drawling, yet venomously. "Lost! I gambled—and lost." Covering her face with her hands, she burst into tears.

What did she mean by "lost"? I was perplexed. How had she "gambled"?

She sat hunched over for a while longer as she continued to weep. Then she smoothed out her hair and wiped the tears from her face.

"A misfortune. Utterly unlooked for," I said, for the sake of saying something.

"No, my friend. It wasn't unlooked for," she said. "From the very first day that I met him, I knew that that's how he would end."

Then a stern, earnest look came into her eyes. They glowed with that fire one sees in the eyes of those who are about to fling the truth into your face.

"I did not love him like a wife," she said. "I lived with him because I hoped to rescue him. If I loved him at all, it was because he was unhappy. Misfortune moves me. The first time I ever saw him, he was weeping as he looked into the eyes of a horse that had collapsed in the street. I remember that when the horse was dead, Vogelnest tried to console the wagon driver and gave him some money.

"I loved him then, and I had a dark inkling that things were very bad with him. Then, by coincidence, we met, and on that very first day I knew that he could not live long. That he was weary of everything he had ever seen in the world. I left home. I left my parents and I married him in order to keep him from . . . to . . . It was a gamble, my friend, and I lost."

She stared straight before her. The rays of the cheap lamp were refracted in her eyes and glistened in her tears.

I remembered the moment on the stairs when she had laughed down at me. At last I understood what that meant.

31

That same day I went to Katowice with the dark Jew from Komarno. We went half the way on foot and rode the other half. We found work in the coal mines.

Early one morning we were lowered into the depths of the earth.

And snow covered the earth, and us.

Afterword

BY LEONARD WOLF

In the December 1928 issue of *Literarishe Bletter* published in
Warsaw, Sh. Zaromb, reviewing Israel Rabon's *The Street*, complained that it had "hardly any unity. . . . There is no plot compli-
cation, no theme, no subject—and yet, if you open the book, you
have to read it to the end—almost against your will."

The book exasperated Zaromb. "The author," he went on to say,
"handles his materials very carelessly. That seems to be characteris-
tic of him or he would not have let pass such a scandalous number of
printer's errors which warp the meaning of whole sentences. . . .
The entire book is written with an inattentive touch, as it were; with
a hint of impatience, as is indicated by the frequent use of etceteras,
which is considered a weakness in the literary world."

Indeed the physical look of the Yiddish text confirms Melekh
Ravitsh's remark that Rabon "never went to any of the official

• 185 •

publishers [in Warsaw]. His books were printed by corner presses and looked as if they, themselves [like their author], had been sick with smallpox" (Ravitsh, *Mayn Lexikon*, p. 246). Not just pages but chapter headings are misnumbered or not numbered at all. Words are misspelled or missing or defaced.

And yet once Zaromb opened the book he could not put it down. Because everything in *The Street* works. "Once we forget the concept 'novel,'" Zaromb says, "and think only about the concept 'street,' then everything, even the errors, breathes of the street . . . the circus, the movie theater, the hotels and inns, and the people sharing the same psychosis who come and go, never to be seen again. They are all tragic—and they are all the street."

That authenticity, that vitality are still there. Short as it is, *The Street* is a book that is as packed with grotesque people and events as a Diane Arbus exhibit or a collection of tales by Flannery O'Connor. At the center of Rabon's story is the narrator, the recently discharged Polish soldier who seems to have been catapulted from the war (a sort of psychological outer space) onto the continent of postwar Europe. The war had reduced his humanity to a narrow focus—staying alive; in Lodz it is again contracted—to a paltry but desperate search for food and a warm place to sleep.

A contracted humanity *is* grotesque. Which is why the bizarre form of the book reflects its theme. What we have is a cluster of tales whose links to each other are not always immediately clear. But if we think "deformation," the wild shifts in narrative and point of view make sense. The strangeness is meant to work like warped funhouse mirrors that make us wonder who we are. But for that to happen, we have to know what we look like in an undistorted mirror, which is why, I think, Rabon gives us brief glimpses of quite ordinary people: the married woman whose basket the narrator carries; the schoolgirl whose book he picks up; the stagehand at the circus; the frightened young women the narrator pursues.

Almost everyone else in the fiction is out of round. First there is the mad shoemaker who is about to hang a child whom he confuses with the defeated German Kaiser, Wilhelm II; then there is the suicidal poet Vogelnest, and his ambiguously beautiful wife; then the dwarf, Doli, who every night holds death at bay during his performance in the circus. There is Jason, the mountainous and coldly erotic wrestler; and finally, gathered together in the municipal beggars' house, there is an entire sideshow of people out of the lower depths. When the people are not twisted, their adventures are. There is the narrator, whom we see on the battlefield turned into a frozen, bloody cross; or standing behind a movie screen fending off mice with his shoe while he shouts his version of the French Revolution to an audience of weavers on strike. Finally there is the tale told by the man from Komarno of his wanderings across Russia and China.

Rabon's people, though they feel very much alive, are not very subtly imagined, because he is not making a study of individual human nature. For his design, it is perfectly appropriate for them to be caricatures, though his early critics, put off by so much strangeness, complained that he was superficial. N. Veynik, in *Oyfkum* for January 1930, said that "Rabon never gets below the surface . . . he gathers a good deal of anecdotal material but he does not synthesize it." Depth of character is not the point here, because, despite Rabon's naturalistic manner, *The Street* is not a study of individuals as much as it is a map of feeling; and maps are all surface. What we have in *The Street* is a revelation of the way things felt, rather than how they were, during the hallucinated years immediately following the Great War.

Rabon recreates on an intimate scale the state of shock that World War I induced on the psyche of the still young twentieth century. Y. Y. Trunk (*Unser Tsayt*, June 1958) says that Rabon's protagonist "has finally deeply recognized mankind. He got to know him on the bloody battlefields. In the black wastes of night, in the course of hand-to-hand combat, where, like roaring bloodthirsty beasts people slaughtered each other . . . the spilled blood exciting their true instincts. . . . On those fields of slaughter man divested himself of every self-flattering mask of culture and morality. He stripped himself naked of all his acquired deceptions. There he revealed himself for what he essentially was: an eternally bloodthirsty beast." But it is not just the battlefield that counts here. Indeed, the battlefield is but a small segment of *The Street*. The shock of recognition the book creates goes beyond the discovery of human bloodthirstiness. What the book regenerates for us is the clamminess that settled over every Grand Illusion after the orgy of slaughter ended.

Rabon was not the only one to be dismayed, or the only one to turn his dismay into a work of art. His world as we see it in the streets of Lodz is different in every way from the one in which Jake Barnes lives in *The Sun Also Rises*, or the one we find in Eliot's *The Waste Land*; but the differences are accidental, not essential. The voices of the authors are different, as are their angles of vision, but when we follow their glance we find the same dazed world in whatever direction we look.

The details of poverty that Rabon describes in his two novels, *The Street* (1928) and *Balut* (1934), derived from his own experience. He was born in 1900 in the Polish village of Govorchov in the Radomir district and was named Israel Rubin, the name he kept until he began his career as a writer. Then, when his work was confused with that of another Israel Rubin, he chose to call himself Rabon.

His grandfather on his mother's side, Israel Revisorski, was a wedding jester with some local fame as a writer. Rabon's father was an educated man who chose to outrage his family by becoming a wagon driver. Rabon was still a small child when his father died, leaving his mother to raise her four children alone. When the boy was two years old his mother left Govorchov and took her children to Lodz, a textile manufacturing city which had in those years a population of more than 130,000 Jews. The family settled in Balut, the most poverty-ridden district in Lodz. Israel Rabon was one of approximately a hundred children who swarmed about the compound on Fayfer Gass where the family lived. Most of the children, the young Rabon included, grew up without much care.

His mother, who never worked herself out of the Dostoevskyan poverty into which the death of her husband had plunged her, made a living as a used goods peddler. Fayfer Gass was as low down in the social scale as anyone in Lodz could get. It was, says Yosef Okrutni, who was a friend of Rabon's, a street of acrobats, organ grinders, ragpickers, professional invalids, and prostitutes (Okrutni, *Zukunft*, November 1973). But it was also the street on which the secondhand dealers' union had its social center. There, there were lectures, classes, and poetry readings that the boy Rabon, encouraged by the social activist Yosef Morgenthaler, occasionally attended.

One can only guess at the real texture of Rabon's life in those years, but many of the details we have are grim. His mother left the house early and came back late from her peddling rounds. His older brother, who had become a weaver, was arrested for political activity and exiled to Siberia. From there the brother fled to the United States, where he was lost to sight.

That was one disaster. Not long afterward, Rabon's older sister took what Khaim Fuks calls "the slippery path" and also left home. As for the younger sister, as soon as she was able, she joined her mother in the secondhand business, and the boy, Israel, was on his own.

And yet his childhood had its lighter moments. Yosef Okrutni tells us that Rabon's sister Soretshe, the one who took the non-slippery path, married a man who lived in the vicinity of the Flora Theater, in which "cheap melodramas were played in Yiddish: The star of the theater was Regina Tsuker. In the course of a scene in one of her performances she removed her clothes . . . while she sang teasing couplets" (*Zukunft*, November 1973). The young Rabon sneaked into these performances. On one occasion he was present when a nursing mother in the audience, irritated because her child refused to take the breast, cried out, "Take it, you little bastard. If you don't, I'll let him have it [indicating an actor on stage]."

In the Flora Theater, Rabon got one part of his education. Another part he derived from his nights of reading in a bed that was surrounded by his books and by the rags and feathers that were the debris of his mother's business.

Poverty-stricken, more or less self-taught, and intellectually ambitious, Rabon started his writing career early. He was fifteen when he published humorous verses in Lazer Kahan's *Lodzer Folksblat*. Then, for a time, he wrote a column called "Shrapnel," which he signed with the first of what would later be a great many pseudonyms: Little Israel.

He became interested in European literature early on. We know that he translated poems by Rilke and that he managed to study French with the help of Shimon Shpigl, another Lodz writer. Rabon not only read but also translated Villon, Baudelaire, and Rimbaud. *The Street* shows traces of that French reading in the strained loftiness of the death-loving prose that the suicidal poet Vogelnest employs in his fragment of a novel, *There*.

Clearly, Knut Hamsun's *Hunger* (1890) is the formal model for *The Street*. Even if we did not have I. B. Singer's authoritative assertion that "the whole modern school of fiction in the twentieth century stems from Hamsun . . . [and that] Hamsun even had an effect on Hebrew and Yiddish literature," we would need only to glance at the two books to see how Rabon derives from, though he finally does not imitate, the Norwegian master. Both books have alienated protagonists who move about in a large city while their fortunes go from worse to appalling. Both men have weirdly inconclusive relationships with women. And yet, though it is possible to point to individual scenes in Rabon that recall moments in *Hunger*, the two books, both in their scope and their effect, are worlds apart. *Hunger*, as Robert Bly points out in the introduction to his translation of the book, describes a journey into the abyss of an individual psyche. The protagonist's physical hunger serves, by heightening his senses, to equip him to make that interior journey. Rabon's narrator, on the other hand, has his eyes almost entirely on people and events outside himself.

Early reviewers of Rabon's first book of poems, *Behind the World's Fence* (1928), were quick to point to the influence of Moyshe Layb Halprin on the young poet. He was, in Yitshak Goldkorn's phrase, *"Moyshe Laybik roy"* (raw Moyshe Layb). But Halprin, as the remark suggests, is altogether a more complex poet—and one, moreover, who in his poems of grief and solitude manages to create a persona in whom one can take some interest. What Rabon's *Behind the World's Fence* mostly reveals is a poet still learning to fuse his feelings with his craft. In the poem "I Am" he writes:

Within the storm, there's me. I'm wild; I'm black.
I fly in all directions, like the wind,
And there's a heavy sorrow always in my heart.
And always there's a flowering field in me.

In me the wild and panting laughter of debauch,
In me the pure clear brightness of a mother's tear,
In me the roaring scorn of one who wields a blade;
In me a devil dances, yelling with desire.

I drag my day by the horns the way one drags
An untamed ox whose sparkling joy, whose flame is spoiled;
Then weary, raw, and sated I turn back
To my dark and dancing solitude again.

Rabon is at his best in *Behind the World's Fence* when, as in *The Street*, he is most direct. In his "Prayer for Rest," for instance:

God!
You have seen the sun go down in me;
You have seen my blood asleep in me.

You have seen how my heart weeps in me.
You have seen the world complain in me.

You have seen how joy dies out in me;
You have seen Yourself decline in me.

. . .

Ah, let me rest and take my heart to You.
And let my soul rock gently to its death for You.

Poetry is the high road to Parnassus, but rent money is hard to come by there, so it should not surprise us that Rabon, who was perpetually poor, should have diverted some of his abundant literary energy to the task of making a living. When he was not writing poetry, his pen was for hire. Melekh Ravitsh tells us that "Rabon balked at no writing job whatever. He wrote trashy novels and detective stories and bragged about doing them. And in that domain he was much in demand. . . . But he rarely sold anything to what one might call the respectable press" (*Mayn Lexikon*, p. 248). For the *Lodzer Tageblat* and for *Haynt*, Rabon wrote dozens of potboilers under a variety of pseudonyms and he recast German and Polish fiction into Yiddish.

When he was in his early thirties he moved to Warsaw, where for a while he edited the monthly *Oys*, in which he published poems, stories, and essays under his own name and under the pseudonym of Ruth Vintsiger. Melekh Ravitsh describes the mature young Rabon as "thin, very thin, slightly taller than middle height, blonde; always slyly smiling, and a bit suspicious, but certain that one could not pull the wool over his eyes. . . . [He had] a deeply pockmarked face, and suffered because of it; certainly the development of his soul was affected by it; and therefore the character of his writing (*Mayn Lexikon*, p. 246)."

Rabon's second novel, *Balut*, was published in 1934. A study of the lowest depths of poverty, it is set in the same squalid section of Lodz where Rabon grew up. *Lider*, a second collection of poems, was published in 1938 and was awarded a prize by the Warsaw P.E.N. Club.

Rabon was living in Lodz again when in 1939 the Germans came. He made his way briefly to Bialystok and from there to Vilna, where he edited *Unterveg* with Y. Y. Trunk and Noakh Prilutski. Rabon's last literary work of which I can find any account was published in *Unterveg*. It is a chapter of a novel-in-progress that was to be called *The Way to the Stars*.

He was seized by German troops in 1941. As with millions of others who perished in the Hitler years, there is no known date of his death.